HAPPINESS AND OTHER DISORDERS

HAPPINESS
and other
DIS**O**RDERS

{ *short stories* }

A**H**MAD SAID**U**LLAH

KEY PORTER BOOKS

Copyright © 2008 by Ahmad Saidullah

All rights reserved. No part of this work covered by the copyrights hereon may be reproduced or used in any form or by any means—graphic, electronic or mechanical, including photocopying, recording, taping or information storage and retrieval systems—without the prior written permission of the publisher, or, in case of photocopying or other reprographic copying, a licence from Access Copyright, the Canadian Copyright Licensing Agency, One Yonge Street, Suite 1900, Toronto, Ontario, M6B 3A9.

Library and Archives Canada Cataloguing in Publication

Saidullah, Ahmad
  Happiness and other disorders / Ahmad Saidullah.

ISBN: 978-1-55263-959-7; ISBN-10: 1-55263-959-2

1. Title.

PS8637.A446H36 2008   C813'.6   C2007-901831-9

ONTARIO ARTS COUNCIL
CONSEIL DES ARTS DE L'ONTARIO

The publisher gratefully acknowledges the support of the Canada Council for the Arts and the Ontario Arts Council for its publishing program. We acknowledge the support of the Government of Ontario through the Ontario Media Development Corporation's Ontario Book Initiative.

We acknowledge the financial support of the Government of Canada through the Book Publishing Industry Development Program (BPIDP) for our publishing activities.

Key Porter Books Limited
Six Adelaide Street East, Tenth Floor
Toronto, Ontario
Canada M5C 1H6

www.keyporter.com

The line of poetry that appears on page 131 in "The Guest" ("Spairges about the brunstane cootie, to scaud poor wretches") is from "Address to the Deil" by Robert Burns.

The line of poetry that appears on page 131 in "The Guest" ("'O, lay thy loof in mine, lass, in mine, lass, in mine, lass'") are from "O, Lay Thy Loof in Mine, Lass" by Robert Burns.

The lines of poetry that appear on page 131 in "The Guest" (O, my love she's but a lassie yet, my love she's but a lassie yet...) are from "My Love, She's but a Lassie Yet" by Robert Burns.

Text design: Marijke Friesen
Electronic formatting: Jean Lightfoot Peters

Printed and bound in Canada

08 09 10 11 12 5 4 3 2 1

CONTENTS

Editor's Note   /9
Vatan and the Cow   /25
Flight to Egypt   /34
The Wounded Tree   /58
Fifteen Sketches of Rumi   /69
Book Review   /109
The Guest   /114
The Sadness of Snakes   /135
Whiteness   /159
The Blinding Darkness   /221
Happiness and Other Disorders   /244

My hundred-tongued perjury.
PAUL CELAN

EDITOR'S NOTE

Herroner, the wife, insists that I have this in; otherwise, she'll put me in a sling.

I had travelled to Sulaimsarai on the outskirts of town to give Father Eugenio the news. A Sister Dorota took me to the classroom. The padre was in front of the blackboard teaching a moral science lesson to his students.

"A habit is a hard thing to break. See," he fluted with a groundswell as he erased a letter on the blackboard, "if you remove the 'h,' still 'a bit' remains; if you remove the 'a,' still the 'bit' remains; and, if you remove the 'b,' 'it' still remains. Mukul, I'll come and give you one on the head if you don't behave..."

When he saw me in the doorway, he came forward.

"Do you have a minute?" I asked. "It's about the trunk."

He nodded.

"What did Wordsworth mean by the 'child is the father of man?' Write on that for the rest of the period. I have a visitor."

Later, when we sat in the canteen, I told him the news.

"Just papers?" he asked in his mournful basso. "Are they valuable? Are you sure? Wasn't there anything else?"

I could see that he did not believe that the lot was worthless papyrus. I mentioned that there were claimants to the box. The padre immediately lost all interest and went back to class.

A word, then, about the box.

Call me a collector of foibles and fables. Call me a bookseller, an editor, a publisher, a dabbler, a trinket buyer. Even call me a keeper of secrets but don't call me much of a businessman. It's not surprising to my janno and perhaps to me that, given my generosity, my publishing business is dying, sad to say, to the fall of recriminations uttered by the relatives of my sensible and utterly wonderful wife. She is reading this, of course, and agrees. [Nonsense. I am not and I don't. Why does he write like that? All that flowery prose. Such a lot of gas. Typical.]

Yes, as I was about to say, before my wife interrupted me, I've sold crystal walking sticks, manuscripts, ancient gold plate, gems, gold mohurs to H.P. Kraus in New York and others, I have strolled through the rooms, stuffed with bullion, in the Nizam of Hyderabad's palace; I have handled many curiosities and mysteries in my time but I'm still wary of strangers bearing gifts, the minimifidian that I am. Why I am writing all this is because I got this present, or so it seemed at first. It came into my possession briefly after our town was torn apart by religious violence somewhen in the 1990s, but I amn't sure exactly of the year. The hair turns grey, the memory fades, hélas. For those of you who are curious, consult a gazetteer for our annus horribilis. Go on. Let me have my tea.

I had just ended a phone conversation with a certain Ceri Kirwan, the daughter of Cyril and Stella Fielding—she had finished this book and called me from London to offer me her parents' papers from Alipore for a consideration—when Father Eugenio brought me this unprepossessing black metal trunk. Unprepossessing despite its size because, seen from the outside, it was nondescriptively rectangular and large and set with huge flanges but incredibly, incredibly heavy; so heavy that ten labourers from Bhilaspur were bowed under its weight as they dragged it into the verandah. The cast-iron rings on the sides were stiff with age. We walked around it a few times, and it gave me that strange feeling—don't laugh—as if it was some more famous black something in other places but not flying through space or without the drapery and the mumbo-jumbo and bowing and scraping. It had accreted the same kind of mystery to itself.

This container spanned eight feet in width and was four feet deep. Later, it comfortably accommodated my wife standing up in her socks, so it was at most four feet high. Two strands of metal piping ran as braids round the sides, and the lock looked almost cartoonishly designed for a treasure chest. It had been copper chased with faint engravings of wreaths, serpents, dragons, mermaids and schooners, but I could not imagine such a cast-iron chest on even the most outlandish pirate galleon unless it had functioned as a safe. The manufacture was certainly unusual and, although I enlisted many in shifting and turning it, nobody was able to find any maker's marks on it, or any kind of imprimatur.

Anyway, it looked unlike any chest that I had seen, and my guess, the more I examined it, was that it had been custom-built as a strongbox. The tongue flap had acquired the green patina that looks so fetching on roofs and domes but, coupled with grime and what must have been smoke discolouration, it felt hard and greasy to the touch, almost chitinous, like polished wood but with a little more give when one pressed the encrustation with a fingernail. No, there wasn't a key, and the surprising thing was that it didn't carry any suggestion or trace of having been forced, at least not for years.

Under the grime on the top in a raised inset were more arabesques and curlicues and a kind of meander that suggested a West Asian design, which may have explained the words in the vaguely Nabatæan- or Cyrillic-looking runes, yours truly being a specialist in neither. Examining it closely, I could see that parts of the trunk seemed to be older than the rest, although I could not find any joins or welding marks or seams of any kind. Perhaps it hadn't weathered evenly in its exposure to the elements or to whatever forces that had visited it. There wasn't any blistering or flaking as is common with paint, but on the top someone had used a sharp enough point to score out names in spiky letters, male runes that are commonplace nicknames but taken together they stirred memories of my time with the Ashfaq family, on whom more later.

Anyway, a curious present, one'd think, from such an outlandish bearer. The priest was famous for his trips to save fallen women, and for rescuing children from the sex trade, and for some of his own victims who suffered his heavy hand and from the terrors of a ramagemeal hell that he orated on most frightfully in his sermons at the carpentry school, which he ran in Sulaimsarai whenever he felt like it. A tall, cadaverous prelate with a huge appetite, he seemed a larger-than-life figure. These days, he spent the better part of his time with a doctor, who shall remain nameless, organizing adivasis against the higher-caste landlords, but was also known never to have been caught in the middle of any altercation or even a dispute. An agile, labile priest.

I didn't ask the padre about this trunk, not right away. I rarely do in such cases. If you have the instinct to remain silent, secrets will reveal themselves. This is all the more so when they repose in a Goan priest given to maudlin recollections when plied regularly with cups of feni. Obviously, I couldn't do that at home without risking the kind of pyroclasm from my wife that would have re-covered Herculaneum ten times over, servants being the gossips that they are, so I took him to a back room in one of these so-called cafés that have sprung up in our neighbourhood. It didn't take long to get him going. After his fifth glass of rum, feni being unavailable, he sobbed openly about the horrors he had seen in the religious troubles, about his terrified congregation and his brothers and sister, and whispered if I knew anyone who would help them move to Canada or Australia. I was not unsympathetic. England was too anti-papal for their tastes.

At the same time, you can imagine that I was impatient to hear the details of what he had brought. Did he know what was in it? But, by this time, my interlocutor's words and thoughts had begun to deliquesce with drink, and he started to sing snatches of some konkani folksong (one was from that film *Bobby*) in his booming bass. Swift action was clearly needed. I had to talk to him in a quiet place but first I had to hush him. I thought I'd get around this by feeding his other weakness: fish curry and rice. I managed that by tempting him by his nose to walk upright to a seafood shack. After inhaling the meal with a few breaths, he said that it would have been perfect if I had included sorpatel in the bill of fare but, anyway, the realization of that absence seemed to have sobered him up enough.

No, he didn't know whose it was, but he was willing to go halves. Why bring it then, why not take the whole thing for himself? The church would put him under opprobrium for goods taken from a religious riot. Ah, a riot. Which one? Where? Whose trunk? How? Nothing, of course, except more lashings of Old Monk's, which tallied up to two bottles of all the persuasion he could drink. So why hadn't he reported it? For the same reason, and the church did not want to be seen to be taking sides in Hindu–Muslim disputes. We live in fanatical times.

Forget *in vino veritas*, that sacrament of truth. There is nothing so devious as a drunk, except a monk drunk on Old Monk, and even a moralizing drunk monk—I could go on— but I got a sense that one of his parishioners had taken the trunk at the time of the troubles but had been killed a few years later in another "disturbance," as he put it. He hinted that the chappie was a convert whom he had employed at the carpentry school since he was a boy. The "johnny" was confused and distraught when he had joined but had shown talent with wood, he said. He had made all kinds of ornate stocks for guns that they sold to Ely's, the gun and cartridge makers, but kept getting pulled into "wrong ways" by others. Beyond that, his lips were sealed. This person's identity was protected by the sanctity of the confessional, he said and so on. (It was easy guesswork later, though: surely this must have been Munna who used to work at the Ashfaqs and whose sad fate chronicled in 'Flight to Egypt.'")

Frustrated with this drunken catechism but taking care to push down my access of annoyance, I asked him if he knew what was in the trunk. He shook his head mournfully as if he suspected me of double-dealing already. I could sense that he thought I was pushing too hard but he was right. I wanted to know what was in there. We would open it together tomorrow, I said, list the contents and value them, and then decide how to proceed. If there were valuables, I said I would need time—maybe a week, a month, who knows—to trace their provenance, and maybe even contact their owners, if they could be found, and return the goods. He nodded doubtfully over this and was going to protest but didn't. He hinted that he didn't have a place to stay for the night. I had expected that and, since there wasn't any shortage of room, I put him up. As it turned out, he was there for a week before my wife returned.

A locksmith was fetched the next morning but, after pulling the shackle and greasing the post and keyhole and trying various keys that always butted the wards, he left, shaking his head. We then set to with an awl, a crowbar, a hammer, and later even an auger, all suitably very high-tech, of course. The lock seemed virtually indestructible. Finally, we sent for this cashiered shipbreaker from Alang who came with his blowtorch, but it had rusted and he spent an hour cleaning and oiling it before it would work.

"See," he said, pointing to the trunk, "it's been in the fire already but it didn't buckle. Fine work, better than the hulls on many ships."

He blew into the nozzle and then bore into a flange until the metal grew incandescent and the sparks flew off his mask. The Alangi poured water over the metal, which hissed into steam, and it took more than six hours before we could touch the case with cladding without flinching. Then we prised the lock open with the crowbar, taking care to keep away from the still white-hot metal. It gave with a groan, with the anguished sound that metal gives after centuries of rest, or do I mean rust.

When we used rags and towels and beams to raise the lid, I was surprised to see how shallow the interior was. It ended above the top-braid mark. The same conjecture crossed our minds. There must be a false bottom or maybe more than one. Who had made this, where, and how could we access it? You'll say to yourself, "What is Sami rattling on about in so many pages? Was there anything in the bloody trunk or not?" You must allow a narrator his few pleasures, most of which at his age are spent or delayed. I choose the latter but you remind me of my wife. She is equally frustrated with my approaches. "You take too long," she always says.

Let me just say that there were a few trinkets, charts, and the like, blackened with age, fire, who knows, some metal necklace, the one that old Eugenio pocketed "for my school," until I told him I wished he would stick to our agreement. He looked sorrowful at this reproach and gave it back and expatiated on his good and well-meaning motives, which I let pass. You have to pick your battles. But I keep getting interrupted. Let me get back to the topic. Hold off the questions, please.

Our suspicions were right. There was a bottom but when we removed the top tray with its bric-à-brac—I, taking care with my back, it being fickle and prone to collapse under the slightest strain—we found the lower one empty. There was obviously another false bottom as this was quite shallow, just about ten inches to fathom. I got the ten labourers to tip it over slowly, as I looked for a keyhole or a lever or a switch or a hasp, which was quite an operation and the dent in the floor bears witness to this day, but there was nothing although I heard items tumbling inside. As we gave up for the night to avoid any breakage, Father Eugenio drew his cot closer to the box after slamming it shut and proceeded to snore away the effects of the rum.

Needless to say, the next day and the days after produced nothing except more feni and rum, rice and fish curry, and still more drunken yodelling but nary any revelation nor sorpatel. In the end, the padre refused to have the shipbreaker dismantle the piece. He bound it with a cord, promising to get in touch with me, and left with uncanny timing just before my wife returned. I, of course, bore the duty of paying the workers for the good of my immortal soul, as the padre had bargained with all his oleaginous guile.

Needless to say, my wife was curious. *What is it? Whose is it? What is in it? Why don't you open it? What's the secret?* Being a reticent man, the very soul of discretion, old clam lips himself, I demurred and kept on writing my impressions and continued my work on the hidden forms of the divine in Shamshuddin's calligraphy. But who could have resisted the force of Mount Etna when her magma, the lava, and the ash, chose to erupt over the unsuspecting dwellers? She had already begun to smoke. When she reaches that stage, she's unstoppable. It only follows then that some of the secrets of the box were unlocked manually, others by detection, some by chance and some, most fortuitously, by my wife.

I deduce now that she had read my diary on some pretext or the other, being a great burrower into other people's needs like a true spermophile, about the section on the mensurations, particularly the height of the box, and became curious to discover if indeed that it was as I said. She must have unbound the hulk somehow. While I was resting an icepack on my back, eyes closed after a nauseating aqua-therapy session at the Willingdon Club, which had rampant eighty-five-year-olds sashaying to doo-wop in that filthy pool, I heard her muffled, "Sami, Sami." I sprang to the rescue, cursing my twinges. The lid had probably closed on her when she had jumped in, and the final false bottom had probably given way through some kind of elaborate spring mechanism, which must have somehow invaginated up the sides.

After upbraiding me for being so slow to respond to her and not caring for her at all, my fubsy one stood up as tall as she could, tried to peer over the box at me, and said, "I'll help you, you and your precious books," and took out as much of the stuff on the bottom of the box as she cared to and slapped them into my grip.

"There, I hope you're satisfied. I've solved your precious mystery in one go. Easy, peasy. Don't say I don't do things for you."

I thought I saw more papers and two largish boxes to the side, but her ten-minute curiosity span was over. She jumped up to place her feet on my shoulders, her hands clutching my hair, despite my entreaties, and hopped out. Suddenly, the seal closed with a clang. I persuaded her to hop on it a few times more, but nothing happened. That was it. Damaged as I was, I considered joining her but decided I could tango better when my piriformis was snappier. We were never able to open it again. Who knows what lies there, still waiting to be read or thumbed through? Maybe there's nothing.

I'm not the kind who lies through his dentures. Of course, there was something and their discovery in this mysterious box has enabled me, the "editor," yes, yours very truly, to reconstruct the secret lives of a group of characters associated with the Ashfaqs, an upper-middle-class Muslim family who had lived in our small town in north India. I knew them very well. I had published Mr. Ashfaq's poems a long time ago; he was a close friend. My wife had tutored his flighty daughters, Raheela and Selma, for a bit, and even coached Raheela's daughter Mona when she was a teenager before they had all dispersed to the four corners of the world. It's an Indian disease, this endless Linnaeus-like parsing of family trees.

AHMAD SAIDULLAH

Mona had claimed the box as belonging to her paternal grandfather but she returned to me some stories for publication. I got some others from Sultan Amin, our esteemed pleader, who was the legal executor of the Ashfaq estate and had to dispose of the household effects, according to his instructions, after the sad fate of his clients in the riots. There is a third source that you may have guessed. Without my knowledge, my wife has sneaked some of my own writings into the manuscript that went to the publishers, solely to embarrass me. Frankly, I don't have the courage to remove those that she had sent in.

I have presented the stories as I found them. I should be precise. In some cases, I have presented them as they have been edited even if I know that some of these emendations were later, spurious, certainly not holograph. I am sure the true stories of some lie a layer or two below the surface that I have shown you. Some of the narratives are clearly untenable, if not impossible.

Each is written in its own way but by whom? My wife has her guesses, and of course I, being the faithful spouse, concur. All it takes is a little detection. Bring out your deerstalker and your magnifying lens. We have nothing to hide. Anyway, it should please you to know, finicky as you people are, that I've done my best to preserve the authenticity of the papers which were sent to me for publication.

My own contributions to the book of "papers" have been minimal, devoted as they are to recovering the original texts with a view to restoring a diplomatic recension for publication, which has proved to be mostly quite successful, as you well know, given all the cruces. There were hapaxes and haplographs galore in the manuscripts and typescripts to keep me busy. Honestly, I have eased myself out of the work as much as I could, if not to the extent of paring my fingernails, being a self-effacing sort, but there may be a few touches here and there, which are betrayed in an occasional heightening of colour or in a well-turned phrase or trope. Sometimes, writing is irresistible.

M. Samiullah
Editor in Exile
Poste Restante
Gjirokastra, Albania
(Address unavailable to wife, creditors, and critics)
10.V.2007

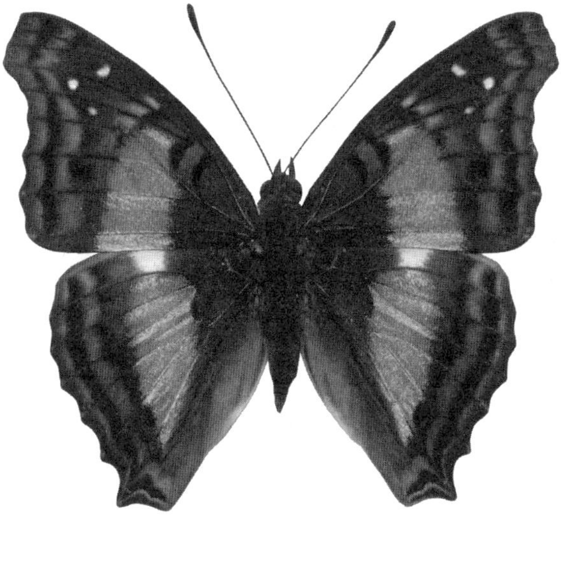

VATAN AND THE COW

It happened in silence, except for the motorcycles, which throbbed in front of the hut. Vatan got up slowly, his left knee aching as it always did in the early morning. Outside, his wife leaned against the cow near the hitching post, red-eyed and silent. His widowed daughter, Gomti, stood in the compound with her daughter, Ganga, who cried in fits.

There were two, then one more, and another later, four men in all. They searched in silence. Vatan knew they were looking for his son, Vivek, but they did not ask him anything. The first man emerged from the hut, gesturing "nothing." One signalled with his head for Vatan to stand away. A small crowd gathered to watch.

The men began to throw their belongings from the hut. The radio, the black and white TV, and the vase landed, cracked and useless, on the stony ground. Clothes, food, pens, school books, mattresses, his walking staff, a scythe, cooking pots, slippers, the paan box, shoes, oil cans, milk cartons, a winnowing pan, quilts, the flail, trunks, plates, chairs, holdall, tumblers, pillows, blankets, and cots soon lay in the dirt. The women picked up the items, shook the dust from them, and ordered them in a pile on the grassy verge.

Vatan turned to the verandah of the big house where they stood. He held his ears crosswise and did a few squats. He then fell on his knees, hands clasped, and looked up in supplication.

"Maharajah, maharani, punish me for any transgressions any way you like but please don't do this, don't throw us out of our home, please," he pleaded.

Their silence cut him to the bone, as if they had turned to stone and he did not exist. His sahib took an envelope from his jacket and flung it at his feet. Vatan picked it up. Money. By the time he had gathered his dignity and straightened to thank them, the door slammed. They had gone.

Vatan unhitched Gauri from the post. He looked at the men. They nodded. Gomti held her child on her hip. The crowd watched the women carry what they could on their heads. Vatan used the staff to punt his left leg along. The cow ambled alongside, its bell tinkling with each step. It was not until they had reached the trunk road that they looked back and saw the smoke from the bonfire.

They walked west. The old man strapped his granddaughter to Gauri's hump. The sun had burned off the fog and now tipped molten lead on the walkers. Along the way, they ate handfuls of parched gram and stopped at streams to rest, relieve their thirst, or to wash the grime and sweat away. During the exodus, the family was silent and uncomplaining.

Near the tannery outside the town precincts, a group of dogs rushed them. The smell and the barking woke up the child. She screamed in fear. Vatan threw stones at the curs and hobbled after them with his stick. They retreated, yelping and snarling, before turning down an alley. Later, when they stopped in a clearing, Gomti squeezed the warm, frothing milk from the udders and gave it to her daughter and parents.

When they reached Phaphamau, Gomti remembered the trunk, which held her marriage papers, the fortune-teller's chart, and the silver necklace from her mother-in-law. Vatan told her to forget them. He was more worried about the jackals that called in the fields. As darkness approached them near Kausambi, Vatan feared that Gauri's bell would attract them.

They reached their cottage in Sassurkhaderi in the early morning. The child was still asleep. Vatan's wife's feet had blistered, and Gomti's right slipper had broken. Vatan's knee was locked and swollen, and his horny soles felt as if they had been over broken glass. Vatan tied Gauri to the post and lay down. Tomorrow, he would have to find some oilseed cake and grass cuttings for the cow.

The next morning, a familiar face appeared. Vatan's cousin, Jagdeo Yadav, asked after the family and listened in silence to his story. He said that things had been bad in his absence. The crops were dying. You could not plant any more seeds. You had to buy them from the company, but no one could afford those prices. His kinsmen, Manmohan, Amitabh, and Surat, had lost almost everything. Three farmers, including his brother-in-law, had committed suicide last year. They had tried to plead with the seth who sold the seeds for the company, but he would not listen to them. Maybe Vatan, as the head of the family, could talk to him.

After washing at the pump, Vatan walked to the big house. The servant looked him up and down and told him that the seth would be at the panchayat and, after that, at the tea shop. Vatan stopped outside the shop. All conversation ceased when he approached. The seth was inside picking at a plate of sandesh.

"Have you come to have tea with us, Vatan?" Sniggering.

"Sethji, you're our father and mother. My kin and I have lost everything. They've asked me to speak to you about the seeds."

"Chalo," said the seth. "Give him a glass of tea."

The tea seller was upset.

"Huzoor, please. They will burn my shop down."

"Caste, waste is all old hat. One of his sons is an engineer and changed caste by marriage. Don't laugh. It's true, a big man," said the seth with relish.

"No, sahib, no tea," said Vatan.

The shopkeeper relaxed. "I can give him tea in a clay cup. If he wants a glass, ask him to open his mouth and I'll pour that down his throat," he offered. The seth laughed.

"Vatan, go home. I'll come in the evening. I have business here."

"Huzoor." He would ask him about the trunk later.

At home, Vatan found the pujari waiting near the cattle post. He was stern.

"Vatan, your son has violated us. Your family's under a curse. It has ruined our village."

Vatan bowed his head.

"Vatan, that's a fine cow."

"God's grace, pujari."

"Take Gauri on a gau yatra to Badrinath and wash away your sins. Only then will the gods smile on us."

"Badrinath is very far and I'm an old man."

"The seth will not relent until the gods make him change his mind. That is the only way. As proof of your penance, you will give Gauri to our temple when you return."

Vatan lay down on his paliasse and thought about his son and his life. He was full of bitterness.

His wife came to tell him that the seth was outside. He wiped his face with the sash.

"Vatan, she's grown into a fine cow. Will you sell her to me for the price you paid for her?" the seth asked.

"No, I am not willing to do that," Vatan said.

"How about double the price? That is fair, I think."

"No, huzoor, I cannot."

"What price, then?"

"Sahib, I have to take her to Badrinath on a yatra."

"Vatan, at your age? Be reasonable. I am offering you a lot of money."

"Sahib, Gauri is my family. How can I sell a member of my family?"

"The cow is sacred and you're unclean. You offend the gods."

"Sahib, I got Gauri through god's bounty, not any man's. I'm taking her on god's errand. If he is not displeased with that, why should anyone else be?"

"You're a stubborn man, Vatan. Eight thousand is my final offer. Think of your family, if not of yourself. No? Anyway, when you return, come and talk to me."

They gathered for the ceremony. The pandit grumbled about purifying a cow for an impure person. Gauri was washed with holy water and then drenched in milk. Rangoli and henna swastikas decked her forehead, and marigold garlands were twisted round her horns. A mirror-studded purple cloth was spread across her back and a saffron ribband knotted above her tail tuft. Gauri bore the attentions patiently, her head in a bag of oats, tail swishing occasionally.

His wife did not question his decision. He gave her half the money from the envelope. She packed some parched grains and nuts for the journey while Gomti and Ganga stood quietly watching. Vatan made a bundle of clothes and supplies. The village saw them, the old man with his packet, his staff, and his cow, turn to specks against the horizon.

The journey was slow, the sun hot. Vatan asked the way to Badrinath of a policeman who laughed. "It'll take you months, pilgrim." Vatan girded his dhoti and walked, calmed by the bell. He thought of his childhood and of his mother and father. He thought of fields of waving ears of corn and wheat where he and his sisters played. He thought of the river that coursed through the village and sometimes overflowed its banks. He thought of the sweet fruit of trees. He thought of his son and cursed his fate.

The days folded into weeks with the same cadence. Children walked behind Gauri, some trying to pull the teats before peeling away with laughter, dogs barking and advancing until Gauri lowered her horns at them, housewives emerging to drop flour, rice, curds, grain, flowers, even money into the tin cup wherever they stopped.

The landscape changed with regularity. Towns belched smoke and noise before passing into groves and open vistas with the sound of wind and the cry of beasts. He saw suns that grew bloodshot over the stubbled fields and chaffed grain, and moons that uncovered more and more stars. Sometimes, hills appeared and diminished into brush, rivers, or jheels. Through it all, Vatan and his cow moved inexorably on, unaware of the cold, the rain, the wind, the sleet, the heat that stung them. At night, the pair stayed under trees, huddled under gunny sacks. Vatan no longer thought; he simply was.

It was in Muzaffarnagar that he was robbed near a mosque by drunken ruffians. Three scooters blocked his way. A man with long hair and a black-checked bush shirt stood and laughed at him. His mouth was stained with paan. He then opened his fly and proceeded to urinate close to Vatan, who jumped away. The others laughed. They pushed him, asked him to open his bundle, searched him, and took the envelope. One brought his belt whistling down repeatedly with such force that it cut the skin and raised weals on Gauri's flank. Then they tripped the old man into the puddle before racing away, that maniacal laughter streaming in their wake.

Their progress slowed. Gauri began to falter. The wounds suppurated. Bluebottles and flies buzzed as Vatan cleaned the pus and applied the red medicine he always carried. Gauri flinched whenever she moved. Slowly, the wound healed but she still had the scars, that slight limp, and her ribs had started to show.

After two months, Vatan saw the mountains and the snow, and his heart lifted. He saw bullock carts, bicycles, and brightly coloured lorries that said "horn please" as they sped ahead. He made the slow climb on the narrow road with its throng of pilgrims and holy men on foot: infants, women, families, and old men carried on their sons' backs like children. Some touched Gauri for good luck and prayed for fecund fields or for children, others for prosperity.

In Badrinath, with its cliffs and torrents, Vatan visited the temples that would allow him in and repented as the priests demanded. He dipped in the cold holy river, fasted and meditated, recited slokas, mortified his flesh, and collected alms on which he and his cow survived. After a month, he had a dream. His wife spoke of how much Ganga missed Gauri.

Although he was ready to leave, his body and soul were exhausted. He had by now a cough, which sounded pulpy, and pains in both his knees and back. The journey home was fraught with dangers. Lorries laden with devotees flew by on hairpin bends. Once, he saw a bus upturned in a cleft far below. It looked like a toy. The temple priest had warned him to look out for thieves who worked the crowds, but he was not afraid. Vatan did not forget to lay flowers at the shrines along the way.

By the time they reached the plains, Gauri was too weak to continue. She panted with each step. Vatan stopped. Gauri buckled to the floor, her head on her forelegs and, although Vatan stayed with her for eleven days, she did not get up again. She lay supine and stopped eating after the third day. She foamed at the mouth, her eyeballs rolled and her skin trembled. From her eyes ran a yellow discharge. The animal doctor said she was hopeless. She died one night as they slept together, the old man and his cow. He stayed with his hand on her head for hours, lost in thought. He covered the corpse with a gunny sack and started walking without looking back.

Months later, when he returned, hardened and spent, he saw something strange in the twilight. His cottage had been razed. The seth had persuaded the panchayat that Vatan had died unatoned and that his family had to be dispossessed to get rid of the curse on the village. The pujari had agreed. They had torched the hut and ordered his family to vacate the land. His wife, his daughter, and Ganga had been expelled to Bamrauli.

The panchayat had seized the other fields that belonged to his clan. Yesterday, the seth's men had set fire to the millet crop in Amitabh's patch. They had stood, bandannas over their noses, wooden torches burning in their hands, setting the place alight. Vatan smelled the burnt holding. Without feeling, he untied his bundle and walked towards the field in the dark. He lay down in the warm ash, looked up at the stars, and waited for the cold night to descend.

FLIGHT TO EGYPT

He leaped over the wall with his bag and ducked into a shed. He pressed his arm to stop the bleeding and watched the windowpane turn poxy with drops. The face that stared back at him was sleepless, twisted, scratched. *Must get rid of the beard and the gun,* he told his reflection as he wiped his brow. He counted the intervals between the flashes and the thunder. 4–5–9–12–16–19–22. The storm was moving away; the rain abated.

Outside, the shadows stretched and clawed their way across the wet patches of light. Through the sweat and drizzle, he saw the constables standing under the canopy with their lathis and carbines. He heard the tall one say something and the others laugh. Inching closer, he saw the scene reflected in their pupils: the fireworks in the slanted rain and hot wind, and figures setting fire to the shops, dragging the inhabitants out and throwing them on the ground. Then, machetes, spears, mattocks, axes, and scythes were illuminated in their work for a moment as the sky split to the sounds of riotous laughter, cries, blows, moans, and whispered pleas. Fear coated his mouth like chalk dust. Feeling sure that he had not been seen, he edged away.

Tiredness bore his body down but he almost ran towards the station and the clinic, cradling his elbow and putting his weight on his right leg as he sloshed through the water. He knew he had to get away immediately, get to Bombay, but he also knew that he mustn't panic. There wouldn't be any trouble from the police, the politicians had assured them. Everything had been arranged. One of them had offered him arrack but he could not abide the smell. Maybe it would have helped with the pain. Why had they insisted on him this time, not his men? He could hardly refuse. The bait. The photographs and negatives. Where were they? Pray, try praying, *better than a thousand nights*, but the words stuck and would not form.

He knocked on the dispensary door and asked the girl who unscrolled the corrugated-iron wicket for a razor, some gauze, cotton wool, antiseptic, and drugs to kill the pain, the strongest they had. She brought them out—"Codeine," she said—and glanced with concern at his scratched face and the stain on his arm.

"You really should see a doctor. Do you want the compounder? He's here. He can give you morphia. An injection. Wait a minute," she said before she disappeared in the darkness.

Those gentle, brown eyes and that low, soft voice reminded him of her. He winced and weakened but grabbed the items and left some money on the counter without waiting for change. Turning as he sprinted, he saw the girl emerge with a man from behind the beaded curtain and look, bewildered, all around her.

In the lavatory, he tried to take off his jacket but, despite the sweat, the lining was stuck to the sleeve. After soaking the shirt repeatedly with wads until it came loose, he saw that the wound had turned black. He cleaned it as best as he could, applied the ointment, and tore the gauze into strips with his teeth before tying it. He clutched the sink, which was now clogged with his thick hair, after a feeling of nausea and weakness overcame him. He scooped the hair out with his hands and plopped them into the toilet bowl. He drank from the tap and splashed his face. He gulped two of the white capsules and flushed the waste down, taking his time to pull the chain until it had all disappeared. His hands were shaking as he stored the razor carefully and closed his bag. The face in the steel mirror looked drawn and weak without the beard. He was surprised he had made it so far. The run had tired him, his arm throbbed, and soon the drug would have its effect. Oh, for some sleep. Shaking his head, still weak, he told himself, he must eat something. But first there was this inexplicable ache for a cigarette.

Somebody was hammering on the door. He unlocked it. A Sikh turned around and glared at him with suspicion. In front of the station, he saw them with their scythes, tridents, and white marks on their foreheads, but no policemen. Probably at the riot, he thought savagely. Still, he was watchful as he threaded his way to the queue, aware of the world spinning around him. He mustn't miss the train.

The tannoy had crickled and crackled that his train would be on platform five but, as the rain fell against the siding in a cascade, he could not find that written anywhere on the carriages. When he climbed on, he asked two men if this was the right train. They did not answer or even acknowledge him. He felt like shouting, "Do you know who I am? Do you know what I have done? Don't you have any idea what I can do to you? Have some respect."

Stifling his anger, he moved down the airless carriage where the heat bounced off the metal walls. Ahead, there were some soldiers on the top bunks who were chuckling and lifting items from a vendor's basket and passing them around while the boy circled in despair. He panicked. He lowered his head and moved past them towards another group.

"Is this the train to Bombay?" he asked, wiping his face. Fever, now?

Families did not look up from unpacking their bedding and dinner. He glanced at his watch.

"Please, this the Bombay train?" he repeated in a shriller voice. Stay calm, he told himself.

An old man with spectacles and a pigtail looked up and gestured at the train adjacent that showed signs of moving.

"That, Mumbai," he said, scanning him with contempt.

"But they said five," he protested.

The man returned to his book in silence.

Passing the first-class cabin in the sickly light, he caught another glimpse of himself in the glass. The shoulder of his light jacket was torn, and the padding poked through. He could see the discolouration on the arm and the rucksack stain that had grown into a large brown patch. He moved towards the doorway with a sideways gait, keeping his arm cramped to his side and the bag near his feet. He wrestled with the door, moaning once or twice when the hot metal touched his body, but it stuck to the jamb. The handle would not turn and his strength failed. As he wiped the sweat with his sleeve, he noticed that the door on the other side was open. He jumped onto the platform and ran to the end of the carriage while the rain rapped its knuckles on the metal roof.

"Ey, where are you going?" asked the guard when he saw him hop down, duck, and run under the coupling, which was slick with grease and water.

"My train," he gestured.

He raced alongside the track until he felt hands tug and lift him up. His bag waved alarmingly, and a white-hot pain shot through his shoulder socket. He landed in the carriage entrance collapsing on top of other passengers whose weight bolted him upright. After an apology and thanks and watching the train he had left gain speed, he palpated his arm, pulled out his ticket, and, careful to lead with his right shoulder, walked through the crowds looking for his bogie.

He stumbled into a seat. Next to it, someone had placed a money plant in a pot. His body felt hot, his throat dry, and sleep pricked his eyeballs.

"Yours?" he asked.

Seated across from him, a man neatly dressed—a clerk?—with a tilak, oiled hair, and a moustache shook his head.

Bewildered, he asked, "Can't find my seat. Excuse me, Bombay train, no?"

"Bhusawal–Indore Typhoon. That's the Bombay express," he said, gesturing at the train that was flying past on their right.

"But I was on that and they told me this was it."

"No, a lie, a prank. This is the Indore line," the clerk said, his eyes full of humour.

"It's not funny. I must get to Bombay urgently. An emergency. Motherfuckers." He was close to tears.

"Ah. Why don't you take your jacket off? It's very hot."

He nodded and wiped his brow.

He palmed the capsule with the same delicacy that Father Eugenio dressed in his cassock had shown, at his conversion, to placing the stale wafer, and swallowed it. Was it the rites that had led him to this: the dripping sacred heart, the eating of flesh, drinking the blood?

A young man strolled into the cabin, looked at the plant, and rolled his eyes. "Oh, did it pay full fare or did it come in as a student?" He laughed aloud at his own wit and, after looking at his ticket, moved towards him with hard intent.

"This is my seat, *sir*," the young man said.

The clerk hushed the youth and explained the confusion about trains. He told him that there were a couple of seats available in the next cabin. His cousin and his family for whom he had bought tickets had not shown up. The clerk exchanged a ticket with the young passenger, who gave him a sharp glance before his humour revived with another look at the plant.

"Must have come on a discount. Clever," he said with a grin as he moved through the door and turned left in the corridor.

"Stifling," said the clerk, turning to the passenger. The clerk handed him that ticket and raised both hands in protest as he tried to pay him. "Life's full of these. Who knows? Maybe one day, I'll need help."

A man came by to take orders for meals. This woman on the rajdhani heard someone offering blankets at night, the clerk said. She asked how much. When he said "ten rupees," she said, "give me fifteen blankets."

He laughed dutifully. The clerk unfolded the newspaper and offered him a zwieback and tea from a thermos. Too rattled to refuse, his body eased a little as he sat back and ate and drank and talked absent-mindedly about the monsoon and cricket. The rocking and rattling was soothing, but it compelled him to swallow another capsule. The bitterness returned. He propped the window open and gulped the air streaming in. He was bathed in sweat. The clerk switched on the fan and waved the newspaper for a breeze ("this heat") before offering it to him. He declined and said with a groan that he was going out to stretch his legs.

In the toilet, he pulled the flush until the bowl was clean. He dropped the revolver into the hole with a clang but it got stuck. He plunged his hand in and tried to force it down but the opening was too small. He picked up the weapon with his index finger and thumb and shook it, taking care to avoid the drops. He forced the window open with a gasp and dropped the firearm through the bar. It fell with a plunk, and he heard it bounce twice metallically. Gone. He ran the tap and scrubbed his hands with the soap until they were raw. Another anodyne? Hold on. Stay awake. He checked the bag. Yes, the money was still there.

He gathered himself with a deep breath and closed his eyes. He saw the body tumbling, the face in a rictus, hand clutching at the chest where a large stain appeared on the blank shirt, tumbling but never touching the ground, upright and again tumbling, and looping again, all in black and white. A shot, that was all. Death had left him drained and burning. *We all bear our stigmata, our crosses, and there's suffering at every station*, he told himself.

He had been calm then. He had not seen the bayonet but it now lived in his side. He remembered the bodyguard's expression, though, as the bullet shattered his forehead: the eyes crossed with shock, almost comical, the hibiscus that blossomed between his eyes. He remembered his handlers congratulating him. What had they said when they bundled him into a jeep? *A true patriot. We were right to ask for you. The best. A clean job. A politician, such an important figure, that son of a whore. A victory for the cause. Don't worry, we'll take care of the rest of his family,* they had said with a laugh, hands stroking their groins.

They had given him the money. The rest with the photos and negatives would be there on arrival in Bombay, along with a passport and ticket, where he would work in a hotel in Siwa. Why hadn't they taken him to the station? Oh, yes, the riot. Was it all planned? He drew another deep breath. *Close your eyes again. Think.*

Another, earlier. He found his quarry with ludicrous ease. They had called him an "anti-national, a communist." Odd, but he didn't look dangerous. There he was: thin, pale, glasses, a widow's peak, in a blindingly white shirt with some trace of bluing, standing alert behind his office desk. The only evidence of nerves, his quick, short breaths.

"All these years when I've thought of doing it myself, should I be afraid now?" the scientist said, more to himself. "Is that what you are here for? I've been getting the threats, you know."

He nodded in a silence that engulfed them in perfect understanding, a silence that drained the glugging ceiling fan, the blare of lorries and scooters in the street.

"Look," he spoke as if to a child, "Do you want to pray? No? People like you don't, do they? It won't hurt if you do as I say." Pause. "Take a deep breath in and then expel it all. Remember, if there's any air left, it'll be painful and you'll struggle. Understood? Nod. Your specs. Good, do it now."

He went through the drill, putting on his gloves. He remembered how the fingers had drummed on the desk and the right heel thrashed in reflex before the body went limp. Then he had removed his hands. Methodically, he had closed the bulging, bloodshot eyes, tried to push the tongue back, pulled the collar over the throat to cover the bruising, and had laid him down carefully so as not to touch the leg where the man had soiled himself. He had checked the wrist for a pulse. And then he had left.

Back in the carriage, he saw the clerk had fallen asleep using the newspaper for a pillow. He forced the window higher and watched the sunrise blur the landscape as it spun, wheeling away from the train. At the end of the curve, he saw the caboose swing by and the river on which fishing boats drifted like gulls. He could see nets being cast, fanned, and hauled. Finally, he slept. He dreamed he had died. Someone placed coins, which burned, on his eyelids. Women wept near his bier. Then he was surrounded by djinns who goaded him with bayonets. He cried out in pain and woke up. Someone had gripped his arm. It was the ticket inspector. The clerk explained, and the official wrote something on the back of the ticket that the clerk had given him. He put it away in the folder.

"Terrible about this riot."

Was it his imagination or was the clerk eyeing him with suspicion?

"Yes, crazy times. How long to Bhusawal?"

"Three hours."

"Is there a direct train to Bombay from there?"

"No, from Indore. Not sure when the next train comes. Noon, I think. Your best bet is the ticket office. Tell them what happened and ask for a refund too. Looks like we can beat the Australians this time," he said, rustling the newspaper. "That young boy from Bombay—what's his name?—is really good. The best."

When the train restarted after decanting a few passengers, they became aware of the whirring and flurries.

"Oh, a bird. Must have got in when we stopped. I didn't see it."

"It's a sparrow. I didn't see it either," replied the clerk.

The bird was trapped. It flew blindly in a panic, caromming off the window and the door, desperate to escape. They tried to let it out through the second window, but failed. When he tried to catch the sparrow with his hands, it flew up. There was a thunk, a clatter, and a grating sound when the bird hit the fan. It dropped on the seat, neck broken and bloody, eyes milky in death.

He picked up the body, swept the feathers and wiped the blood, and wrapped everything in the newspaper and thrust it out of the window.

"How sad," observed the clerk. "But this is life."

"Trapped alone in a box until you go," he added sourly.

After a while, he napped.

They would have arrived earlier but the train shunted for twenty minutes before the green light lured it into the station. "Indore" was stencilled in black on the ochre walls. He shook hands with the clerk who stood in the entrance as the coolies came rushing towards him.

"No luggage, no luggage. Take his," he said, pointing at the clerk, and nodded his thanks.

He made his way to the office. He pulled the ticket out of the folder, and the brochure fell out. The teller seized the supplement and the ticket with an "ah," his gold tooth gleaming. "Look," he said, turning to his colleagues who had gathered under the fan and thumbed through the photos of the feluccas on the Nile, the sphinx, the serapeum at Saqqara, Giza pyramids, and the belly dancers a dozen times, swearing on each other's mothers and sisters. Finally bored, Goldtooth returned and looked expectantly at him while he explained the confusion. The teller looked disgusted, examined the writing on the back of the ticket, and, in silent fury, stamped out a refund and another ticket.

"There. Four o'clock, platform two," he said, holding up two fingers to make sure. He smiled. "No, no earlier train."

"My brochure."

"Ah, yes, sorry." The teller handed it over and turned back to his colleagues.

He walked out of the station and felt the blast coil about his person. The tarmac shimmered in the heat. Sidestepping the puddles that glinted in the sun, he made for the café with the awning on the street corner. There came a waiter in a filthy white jacket and an equally grimy rag, which he ran over the table. He ordered a dosa, a custard, and a cold coffee, and said no to the flower seller and the girl with trinkets who approached without much hope. They moved to another table.

The boy had crept up without his knowing it. He sat down in the wicker chair across from him and asked with his eyes for the sweet. He pushed it across the table, more amused than offended.

"Where's your family?"

"Dead," the boy said without a pause, pulling a long face and lowering his long kohled eyelashes with such blatantly practised skill that he laughed aloud. The boy grinned, flecks of custard in the corners of his smile. He lapped up the rest quickly, lifted the plate to his mouth, and drained the syrup. Eight or nine, he guessed. Wait, there was a nimbus of white around his irises. Starvation? Worried, he beckoned the waiter, who tried to cuff the boy away with an "Arrey, hut. Bad boy, this."

"No, another dosa, coffee, a custard, and an orange juice. Lots of water."

The man went away grudgingly, scowling and muttering.

"How old are you?" he asked the boy.

"Fifteen." The henna designs on the palm flashed thrice like signals.

The food and drinks came. The waiter stood sneering behind the boy ready to send him off.

"Okay?" he asked. He pressed the icy steel tumbler against his cheek, then his temples.

The boy nodded, absorbed in eating and drinking.

Done, the boy smiled and huddled closer to him, smelling strongly of attar and sweat.

"You like me? I like you."

"What do you want?" he asked, his voice hoarse, his breath scuttling like a rat among the ashes.

"I show you the old town. Good time. Ganja. Opium. Girls, boys. Nice, cheap."

"No. Go away. Now," he muttered in a low angry voice.

"Why not, please, why not? I, very cheap. For you, not so expensive." The hand was stroking his thigh close to his groin. Suddenly, he was aware of the eyes watching him. He lifted the hand away.

"No. Here, take this. Go away." Repelled, he handed the boy some money.

He got up under the waiter's sardonic gaze. His arm throbbed while he fished for change for the tip. Nervously, he left all of it. Walking away, he turned to see the waiter pocket the coins, stare back at him, and spit on the ground. The boy was nowhere. As an afterthought, he rummaged through his bag. The rest of the money was safe. The boy hadn't touched it. He smelled the hot tar as he walked past the clock tower. The smell reminded him of a dog's breath. He noticed the railway shed where the engines stood.

Putting his bag under his head, he slept on a bench in an arbour until the PA system woke him up. His body felt parched and quavery as paper. He carried his bag in front of him as the guidebook had advised. Inside, Goldtooth flashed him a smile and held two fingers aloft. He nodded, raised his own two, and crossed the waiting area to have his ticket examined. He thought he would have to cross the bridge but found the name on the reservation sheet next to the door of the carriage.

Instead of taking his seat, he walked over to the book stall and spent a few minutes scanning the newspapers. A report on the death. A short, accurate description. He checked the platform. It looked safe. He paid for a novel with a picture of a corpse hanging from the rafters on the cover and walked out. He checked his arm in the bathroom. The bleeding had stopped but it still throbbed. Later, he took another capsule with a glass of tea in the canteen and bought a chocolate bar and sun shades.

When he boarded the bogie, he found his seat taken. Annoyed, he removed his shades and asked the passenger to move. The man was thin and nervy. His moustache, a lit green cigarette, and Adam's apple bobbed as he apologized and moved across to the facing seat. The car was full of his coloured, herbal-smelling smoke. He sniffed suspiciously. Hashish? He coughed and struggled to open the window. The man leaned across and opened it after his efforts made him faint. He recoiled from the man's fetid breath.

"Sorry, Turkish cigarette. Want one?" His teeth were black and rotted.

"No, thanks."

The man then flicked the switch.

"Not on. Maybe the fan'll work when the train starts. Aren't you hot in your jacket? Should have gone AC second. Hot, hot."

He did not respond and, instead, pulled out his novel. He saw the man glance at the cover and bite his lip before puffing on the cigarette. He looked up from the book and coughed exaggeratedly. The man grinned.

The signal went. The guard waved his flag and blew on the whistle. The train eased out of the station. The power came on with a roar, and he relaxed. In the fading light, he could see well-wishers' hands and handkerchiefs being waved and tears being dabbed away. Furious and close to weeping, he returned to his book until they had cleared the town, but he couldn't concentrate. He was aware of the man's steady stare.

The scenery unfolded. The countryside with its dusty, twisted trees, herds of goats, small boys who laughed as they threw pebbles at the train, the clanging and lights at a signal crossing and children waving, a few defecants along the track, reappeared with a different cast whenever the train pulled out of a station. The river always lay beyond, shining its dark mirror into the eye of the sky. The chevrons of gulls were stitched on the sky.

He paused to recollect the events. So much had happened that he couldn't get them in the right order. *Somebody is walking on the universe, and it's as if we can hear the footsteps echo faintly, that's all. Are there any footprints to follow, any spoor to track? Can anyone hear me?* He swallowed another capsule.

"Are you sick?"

"No, just a fever. The rains, you know. I'd like to sleep. Maybe that'll help."

When he opened his eyes, he smelled before he saw that the man was very near, almost peering into his face, close to his bag. He sprang away.

"What?"

"You cried out in your sleep. I wanted to make sure you were all right. Are you?"

He watched the man draw his shoeless legs onto the seat and sit massaging his toes as he started on a monologue, his face mobile and eager. The eyes gleamed.

"We're coming to the place where they manufacture shoes," the man said, pointing to a large grey shape that went by them in the dark, adding, "Did you know that this was a village of fisherfolk once?" When they rolled past a large temple lit with lamps and festooned with bunting, he remarked that it had been built on the site of an important battle.

The man spoke of his days in countries where he had worked.

"Ah, well, it's different in the West. Here it's more difficult but in some ways it's easier too. You can walk arm in arm, kiss and hug each other, and nobody will say a word. But the other business. All that has to be secret and indoors. You married?" the man asked suddenly.

"Yes," he lied, "yes."

He could feel the man's disbelieving stare rake over his left hand.

"There you can do it in parks and nobody cares. One, two, three, or more people. I was in Erzurum, Turkey—you know Turkey?—very cold. I was there for a year. You can go to the baths for it. Put your towel over your right shoulder and they'll know. All those sort of signals. Very easy but they don't like Indians. They mistake us for Arabs and they don't like Arabs, you see. Of course, we think they are Arabs and you know we dislike them, too. Isn't that funny? Any children?"

"Yes, three." Lies again.

The man looked angry but quiet. His eyes glowed to a point.

The glare of the sunlight had diminished.

"Nice boys here, if you like that sort of thing. Keep an open mind. They say it isn't normal. It's normal there. It's normal for me. What's normal? Are you normal? Am I not normal?" the man asked, daring contradiction as his voice rose.

Normal, that night in Kalimpong? He had waited in the makeshift room, the walls made from deal wood cartons. He could hear the sighs and moans around him, which tightened his groin. The woman had brought her into the room, a small, frightened child, and had slapped her when she cried. After he had given the woman the money, he tried to calm the girl. She had huddled in a corner, her fists tight near her chin. Her name was Kusum. She had whimpered and shivered with fear and cold as he undressed her and stroked the vaccination scars on her arm, ran his fingers over the ribs on her thin body, and tongued her nubbly breasts.

He had laid her down on the sodden mattress, which squirmed under them as if alive, touched the crease between her legs, the few hairs sprouting like wool, and had taken her gently at first but then with harder, urgent thrusts. She had gasped in pain. When it was over, she had cried, her head on his shoulder. When they had lifted the mattress, they had discovered the frame was crawling with cockroaches. After they had shaken them off together with disgust and laughter, and dragged the mattress to the corridor, her mood had lightened. Before the sky became overcast, a moon had looked down on them. They had talked for a long time as they lay entangled.

In the morning, he had woken up in a fog until he realized that a rain cloud had drifted into the corridor. He was drenched. He had lifted her head off his shoulder, tucked some bills under the pillow, and left her sleeping under the quilt to go into the downpour. He had sat in the station canteen while he waited for the bus. He had watched the man who worked the tables with his two steaming kettles, which he poured simultaneously into customers' glasses without spilling a drop: coffee from one and hot milk from the other. Where was she now, what was she doing? *Probably grown into a raddled, painted copy of that woman, running her own show,* he thought with an ache. He then thought of the other. Those eyes. Brown. That laughter. *I am that I am. Alone. Again. None shall know me. Empty as a husk.*

The train was running closer to the river. The sun had turned the water red. On the other bank, he saw a necklace of lights moving in the opposite direction. *Is there another me on that train looking at this one, abandoned, fleeing, and dreading to arrive?* he wondered.

"Do you have a place to stay?" the man asked.

"Yes, thanks, I'm being met," he half-lied again.

"I have a hotel near the station. You can stay there, cheap. Anything you like. I get all kinds of people. Travellers too."

He murmured his thanks before turning to his book. The man looked angrier.

"Your book. Is it a good book? Is it about killing? What do you do? Have you been to Egypt? I was there too, you know."

Suddenly, his mind was a hair trigger, his body coiled to strike. Why had he said that? He was aware that he was sweating, despite the fan. No gun. Just a razor. The man had pulled his own newspaper out and started discussing the assassination. A reward. I hope they catch him but that fucker got what was coming. They all did. Time to teach them a lesson. Bastards all. Agreed? It's a war, isn't it? Finish it once and for all.

"Where are you coming from?" the man asked.

"Indore. Visiting relatives," he answered.

"You don't sound as if you're from here."

They talked about the rains and mango crop until the man lapsed into a sullen silence. In the shadows, the man's face looked longer, his eyes predatory as a vulture's. *He's waiting for me to stop moving*, he thought. He felt faint and thrust his head out to gobble the air and feel the cat's paw on his face, but the rush of air left him breathless. He got up and stood for half an hour in the corridor, lulled by the rocking clatter of the carriage.

The train ran like a double-bladed scalpel into the darkness, leaving twin incisions in its wake. He returned to find the man asleep. His fists were balled in his lap. Revived and somewhat relieved, he switched off the light. The carriage was wrapped in gloom. In the window, his eyes stared back at him, black, accusing, and questioning. He looked at his watch. The numbers that indicated ten glowed in green. There was still some time. How would they find him?

He yawned and fell asleep with a vision of the engines in the shunting yard, uncloaked from the night and the steam that curled about them like wraiths: hellish machines with metal feet and clanging pulses where devils with shovels fed souls chugachug into red, flaring maws and pumping iron hearts. He dreamed of goats and of little boys with towels over their shoulders and of revolvers in hennaed hands.

The slogans of the tea and biscuit sellers woke him up before they reached the station. After the capsule, the chocolate, which had almost melted in his bag, was rich and dark and sweet in his mouth, the taste of redemption, the taste of hope.

The man was awake.

"You know you'll be safer there. You'd better stick with me. No police."

"What do you mean? Safer? The police?" he laughed hollowly and cleared his throat.

He was aware of the man's scrutiny. Act naturally. His lips formed the words from the prayer but, again, they would not come. *Abandoned again,* he thought bitterly. Was it his fault that he couldn't believe anymore? Why blame him? Faith was given, Father Eugenio had said; it was not a lack. He had tried. What had he killed for, if not to atone? *Save me from the accusers. Send them away. Let someone else judge. Let her. They'll be looking for me,* he guessed. *Will they wait? They had said that the passage was booked for tomorrow. What had they laughed about?*

Then the city began to appear in the dark. The weave of overhead cables, rubbish mounds with rooting dogs, shanties, tenements, the looped entrails of city streets, fuming buses, scooter rickshaws, and cars in the blackening pall. Soon, the train drew into the station and the noises swelled atonally like an awry chorus: announcements over the PA, tea sellers, vendors, coolies' shouts, travellers, and people waiting to greet the arrivals, just a few at first, then thirty deep as the train pulled in.

"Look, come with me." The carid breath left him reeling and weak. The talons gripped his bicep, and he did all he could not to yelp with pain. Shaking the man off, he jumped on the platform and, ploughing through the crush, raced towards the exit. He searched for the faces he did not know, glancing back in terror. The crowd had thinned and the man—the man had disappeared. He walked out into the glutinous, acrid air.

Near the cycle stand, three men walked up to him, hands in their pockets. One talked into a phone, which blinked bluely. Another—he had big ears and a red slash for a mouth—softly spoke his code name. He nodded, shoulders relaxed, and took a deep breath.

"This way."

They had turned towards the taxi rank but were now walking past it.

"Where are we going? Where's the money, the package? The commander?"

"In the jeep. This way."

"What took you so long? We've waited for seven hours. We thought you'd given us the slip."

Something in the wording and the tone made him pause. Were they just angry at the delay? He turned around. The pair was behind him. The backers stood still. One pointed straight ahead reassuringly. The road unrolled ahead like a tongue into the darkness of an unseen mouth.

"Don't worry about your injury. Everything will be taken care of very soon." Had they been told?

There was a tension, a lightness, and a slow, watchful purposefulness that he did not understand. He paused to take out a capsule, which he put in his mouth. The man in the front had disappeared. The two at the rear had melted into the darkness. What was happening? He wheeled in terror.

He started running straight into the gloom, unable to swallow, the medicine bitter in his mouth. He could see the painted white stripes on the road leading into the darkness, and heard the sound of the waters lapping and somewhere a dog barking. He ran harder, with short breaths, leaning on his right side, arm jarred, something dropping from his pocket—yes, the shades—heading into the darkness of the unpaved alley, and felt the stubble under his feet as he almost tripped. He paused. For a while, he thought he had lost them. Then he heard a whistle and voices somewhere in front, the strike of a match, and ahead a glowing point of red and a wisp of green smoke curling against the dark. Steps quickened. There was a movement to his left.

"Come," he heard it, soft and insistent. "Here."

His jacket shone like a flag. Too late to turn, he saw the flash before he heard the thunder, which clawed at his chest, and the second sharp entry through his neck, which shook his breath before he felt the pain and then the oozing warmth. He fell to the ground on the bush and the rubbish pile, the capsule still in his mouth, his nose filled with the smell of rot and sodden earth.

He had a moment of clarity. *I go to my death not as a soldier or an executioner but as a victim, a sacrifice, like him but unknown, unmourned, bound like a beast on an altar awaiting the knife.* He saw the shaven priests with bowls of incense and adzes, the Nile lying sullenly in bed, the wind lifting from a stale censer, the bulls of Apis in their stone graves, bled, the painted sarcophagi, the dark shed, the scuttling of the rats, the sawdust under his feet, the tuck of the scooter, and the laughter of his friends at cricket. He wanted to say, *This is not me, I give up my body, take it, save me, let her, bring me home, the place is rotting and I am sinking,* but they were around him.

"Selma," he cried. "Selma."

"What was that? What did he say?"

"Cried for his whore. Son of a bitch."

A boot thudded into his side.

Someone had opened his bag and was searching it with a torch.

"Couldn't wait to spend the money."

He smelled the herbal cigarette and heard the man complain.

"Almost got away."

"Sisterfucker."

He thought he recognized the speaker. The master's voice, here, but his laugh came out a scarlet gurgle. He saw a light moving away from him; it was getting dimmer. He was emptying; he was far away. He felt faint. The darkness roared in his ears.

How many lives can one have when you are already dead, how many deaths? His last thought surprised him. The man must have knelt and aimed before he shot him. Not dead yet. He tried to swallow the capsule to cut the pain but knew it wouldn't be any use. His mouth lolled open, and it rolled out in a trail of saliva as his senses ebbed and fused with the darkness.

"Oh, look, a pearl."

He did not hear the final shot.

THE WOUNDED TREE

They had smashed the boundary wall a week before his parents arrived. In the morning, Khalid had found the mustard plants uprooted in the muddy fields, rubbish strewn over the flower beds in the courtyard, and the coops destroyed. Dung splattered the boundary wall that was still left standing—they must have used something heavy to knock the rest down—where they had drawn crude sketches and slogans in chalk streaked now with rain.

The police had gone over the scene, prodding with sticks, but did not find any clues. Khalid had not heard the "jagte raho" that night, but Mukund, their old night watchman, in his cottage was helpless. Ramesh, the old man's grandson, who had recruited the workers for the clean-up, claimed that he had heard that Munna Bhai had hired the thugs for Palwalkar the contractor. The workers in the neighbouring huts said they had not heard anything. The large tamarind tree that sheltered the hut had been slashed with a cutlass or a cleaver. The white shone through like bones.

When Khalid's parents came, the family held a council before they went to bed. They were still asleep when Khalid and his brother, Tariq, left at dawn for their morning walk. The birds in the cages in the verandah were quiet. The boys stopped when they saw the crowd: men in dhotis sitting on their haunches under the tamarind tree whose scars had turned brown, sucking on bidis through cupped hands, waiting like vultures for the kill. Wailing came from the cottage. It turned into sobs and coughs. Women stood blocking the doorway, their pallus over their mouths. Ramesh was outside with a mewling kitten in his arms. It called its responses to the laments in a thin, starved tone.

"What's going on?" asked Tariq.

"Sahib, Nanaji very sick."

"He won't go to the doctor."

"The priest is coming," said Ramesh.

Inside, it smelled of cow dung cakes and smoke from the brazier. Tariq saw Mukund's grizzled head dip and rise in the shadows as he struggled for breath. The old man stood at an angle, gripping an upright cot behind him for support.

"Arrey, Ramesh ki nani, get these people away from the door. Give him some air," Tariq said.

Mukund's wife, in her grief, beat away the visitors with half-hearted gestures. Khalid tried to talk to her.

"Arrey, Ramesh, put some butter on the paws. That way it won't run away again," she said as she saw the kitten struggling in his arms.

Khalid spoke. "Ramesh, call the doctor." The boy sped off, legs flashing. The crowd at the vigil grew. Ramesh appeared again after some time.

"He won't come."

They walked down a street towards the cantonment until they came to the concrete gates.

"Get us a rickshaw, Ramesh, will you?" Khalid asked.

They rang the bell later. A short man with curly hair, in a blue sleeveless sweater and tan trousers, stood blinking crossly through his spectacles as he held his hands on his paunch.

"Dr. Gupta. Our night watchman, a patient of yours, is very ill," began Khalid.

"Can't breathe," added Tariq.

"Mukund? Yes, I know. His heart. Cardiac asthma. Bad case. They gave up on him at the hospital last time. I told the boy. Nothing I can do." A low voice on the verge of complaint.

"There must be something," Tariq said.

"A gone case, sir. Take him to the hospital. Get him some oxygen or Ventolin. That's all. I told the boy. Excuse me. My tea is getting cold," Dr. Gupta said.

Tariq was indignant. His tea! Ramesh ran alongside the rickshaw. The early morning signals were sounding: the matins bell at St. Thomas the Martyr, the tinkle from the local shakha, the lowing of cows being milked, the rococo of a distant, laggard cock, and the occasional roar of a lorry rushing past on the trunk road. Khalid told the man to wait as they neared the cottage.

The crowd had grown. Khalid elbowed his way in, scattering the women and girls who were consoling the wife. Faces were quickly hidden behind pallus.

Mukund's wife wiped her face as Ramesh held and patted her hand. She answered in a hopeless monotone. Yes, he had not slept all night. No, he hadn't complained about chest pains. He won't take his medicines. He refuses to go to the hospital.

Mukund's eyes had filmed over. His chest heaved like a bellows. He was curled with the rasps and wheezes that shook his body. His talon-like fingers still held him up. Somehow, he managed to find the strength to shake his head when Tariq entreated him to go to the hospital. He insisted on going to the Diamond Health Clinic instead, his wife explained. They couldn't pay five thousand rupees at the government hospital last time so the doctor had sent them home.

When Tariq returned to the farmhouse he found his parents awake. Khalid was talking on the phone.

"I've explained it to the doctor, you know, Jeejee. He has to go to Kheri on party business. Some trouble between farmers and thakurs. He said to take him to New Yagna instead. Forget Diamond Clinic."

"This is too much. It doesn't stop. I'll ask Billa to send his men again. It's been thirty years: court injunctions, appeals, hearings, postponements. Nine lawyers have died. In the meantime, all this stealing and vandalism's still going on. No law and order in this country. I'll have a word, Hina, with this Gupta fellow also," promised Mr. Hidayatullah with a glance at his wife. "Reasonable chap, I think."

"It's not that. He's been with my family since he was a boy. Even if he's hopeless, the least they can do is to make him comfortable," she said.

Khalid made sure that Mukund and his wife got on the rickshaw. The man's face was creased with exhaustion. He was bent almost double as people supported him on both sides and lifted him on to the rickshaw with an effort that left him holding his head between his knees.

"Rickshewalle, do you know New Yagna Clinic? Good, cycle carefully. Ramesh, phone me when you get there. Number hai, na?"

In the drawing room, Khalid turned to the others.

"Jeejee said that these clinics are all bad. No money, no oxygen treatment. Jeejee knows the Yagna doctor, though. He wasn't sure if he'd be there on Sunday, but he'll call him anyway."

"Fellow's useless. Probably did it himself and faked all this," said Mr. Hidayatullah.

"Daddy, he's over ninety!"

"Too old for this job. We've enough on our hands trying to put this farm right."

"Listen, he was Abbu's old servant. I can't just throw him out of my house," Mrs. Hidayatullah stressed the "my," "now that he is sick, just because you want that. He looked after Abbu, don't you forget it."

"Arrey, Hina, men, don't get so hot. Accha, bhai what's for lunch? What wouldn't I do for your spicy raw kawabs?"

"Jeejee said I should speak to his wife, Shehnaz, while he's away," Khalid interrupted.

"Very nice couple. No airs and graces," Mrs. Hidayatullah added approvingly.

"I need that massage. When does Ramesh get back?" Mr. Hidayatullah asked.

The nurse's call came while Tariq was directing the labourers who were piling the bricks and Khalid was supervising the field clearances.

"Sir, the doctor is not here. No, he won't come today."

"Look, didn't Dr. Jeejeebhoy speak to you? Well, then, what are you waiting for? Tell the matron to give him some oxygen and keep him overnight. We'll send him to the government hospital tomorrow," snapped Mr. Hidayatullah.

The nurse hung up, cowed but grateful.

While Mr. Hidayatullah visited the lawyers and went to the carpenter's to order wood and wire for the chicken coops, the head nurse called and spoke to Mrs. Hidayatullah.

"He's been given oxygen and his breathing has stabilized. We'll keep him here."

After lunch, Tariq was woken by the clamour from the rookery of hundreds of crows over the cottage.

"Get your .22, Tariq. Here's your chance," said Khalid with a grin as his brother appeared.

He gestured at the doorstep where the kitten was sitting with a crow, twice its size, struggling, but clenched firmly in its mouth. The kitten watched the circling birds warily and inched with its prey into a corner of the doorway whenever they dived. But it would not let go. After a while, the bird stopped moving. The crows went wild. A boy wheeling a bicycle rim with a stick screamed in terror after a rook raked his hair and others tried to peck it. His parents emerged with sticks to beat them off and rescued their child.

"The bastards," said Tariq in frustration.

No matter how often he tried, he couldn't hit a single bird. Sometimes, one would drop a feather to show that it had been hit before it would wheel away safely, crowing with derision. Khalid kept grinning. After half an hour, the rooks settled down but their paroxysms of rage resumed whenever the kitten came out. Khalid returned to the removal of the rubble from another section of the wall that had just collapsed.

Ramesh was at the door.

"Aha, come in. I'm waiting," said Mr. Hidayatullah. "What news of Mukund?"

"Sahib, Nanaji died," he said, dry-eyed and calm.

"Arrey, when, how, what happened?" asked Mrs. Hidayatullah in a high voice.

"Heart failure."

"How is it that the nurse didn't phone?" asked Khalid more to himself. "Wait, I'll call Shehnaz. Jeejeebhoy's away but she'll know. She's a doctor too."

"Jao, Ramesh bete, jao. Go, we'll come," said Mrs. Hidayatullah.

Shehnaz arrived at four with her twins, Firdaus and Fakhra, in their school tunics. They sucked lollipops and spent most of their time with Tariq, feeding the finches.

"Eat, Firdaus and Fakhra, come on, these sweets are for him. Khalid's got into the army. He joins up in September. Wants to become a superspecialist in strategy. Infantry side," Mrs. Hidayatullah said as she offered up a box of sweets from Malluram's.

Khalid looked a little embarrassed at the congratulations.

"That tamarind tree will have to come down and maybe the guava grove. We can build the chicken coops there." Mr. Hidayatullah announced the plans.

"Listen, not that tree. I played under it when I was young. It shades the cottage." Mrs. Hidayatullah was firm.

They were discussing ideas for repairs and renovations.

"We must get rid of the rookery. The damned birds eat all the seeds. Nothing grows," Mr. Hidayatullah said.

Shehnaz narrated how, when she was in school, her friends would often sneak into the farmhouse and pelt the tree with stones for the sour, luscious fruit.

"The best imlis in town. Oh, auntie, I went to the clinic an hour ago. He's fine. He was asleep when I got there," Shehnaz said.

"Eh? But why did Ramesh say he was dead? How strange. Call him, Tariq," Mrs. Hidayatullah commanded.

Ramesh looked sheepish as he fidgeted in the doorway, listening to their questions.

"Ji, a crow pecked me," Ramesh explained.

"Auntie, it's nothing, just a silly old superstition," Shehnaz said. "Once that happens, you have to tell everyone that someone close to you has died. Just to ward off the evil eye. Really silly. Auntie, when will you find a girl for Khalid?"

"All that stress for nothing. Crazy," said Mrs. Hidayatullah.

Shehnaz scolded Ramesh gently. She told him that she had spoken to the head of cardiology at the government hospital, and he had arranged a bed for Mukund the next day. His grandfather was well.

"Nani has asked for money for the medicines," Ramesh said softly.

"How much?" Mr. Hidayatullah asked.

"Fifteen hundred."

"What does that woman think? That I have rupees coming out of my ears for everyone?" said Mr. Hidayatullah.

"Listen—"

"Ramesh, what medicines?" Shehnaz interrupted. He gave her a chit of paper.

"These places overprescribe. He doesn't need all these tonics and injections. Just give him five hundred, uncle. That should be enough."

"Ramesh, here. If it's not enough, come back and tell me. Mind you, I need a champi, don't forget. We produce the best doctors in the world but there's no regulation here."

"Arrey, Ramesh, remember to get some more workers tomorrow. There's still a lot of rubbish. Some trees have to be cut."

"Not the tamarind!" Mrs. Hidayatullah was firm in her decision.

The morning was foggy. The brothers were strolling in the cantonment past the polo ground. The road was empty. Khalid saw a couple of dogs copulating. He chased them, and they tried to run apart although they were coupled back to back. A cadet came running in a vest and shorts, a neem twig in his mouth and a swagger stick under his arm. Tariq suddenly turned and jogged behind him, mimicking his crimped elbows and high-stepping gait.

"Are you making fun of me?" the runner stopped and shouted, his face purpling.

"Nahi, bhai, just jogging behind you and admiring your technique," Tariq responded.

Furious, the jawan raced off. Khalid snorted with laughter.

"You'll have to jog in your shorts too," Tariq said.

Tariq grinned as they headed to the south Indian café for a dosa and a coffee. It would be a long, hot day in the fields.

At the house, the Hidayatullahs were talking to Jeejeebhoy, Siddiqui from the police, and Dr. Gupta, whose eyes twinkled behind the lens as he listened. He gave a puff of laughter when he spoke.

"Ah well, it wasn't like that, Hidayatullah Sahib, at all at the hospital. Mukund's wife just thinks that the old man is a gone case anyway, so why bother? Five thousand rupees? That's nothing. She bought her daughter-in-law a sari worth twenty thousand rupees and gave her son a big colour TV and a mobile phone last year. Did you know that? Our servants say that she has a lakh stowed away. It may be less, of course, madam. You're right."

Siddiqui said, "In these cases, the developers were probably paying someone. Who knows who else is involved? Probably some politician or another." He would send a sentry again.

"The lawyers gain most of all," Mr. Hidayatullah said. "We can't build anything. Now it's ex-parté. They claim that the original owner died and bequeathed the property to these developers."

"I have arranged something," Khalid announced. "I have organized others. We'll hold a procession of the dead in Lucknow outside the courts. We will be carried on shoulders in open coffins, and we'll sit up at every hundred yards and call out, 'We are alive.' It'll be big. They'll take notice, the courts, wait and see."

"Accha, these sweets are for Khalid. He joins the army in September. Wants to become a superspecialist in strategy, kyo Khalid? Infantry side, is it? Please have some," said Mrs. Hidayatullah.

A few days later, when Khalid and Tariq rounded the driveway, he was there seated on his cot under the tamarind tree with the slashes on the trunk now blood red. Some of the brown fruit lay heaped on a piece of cambric. The kitten was pawing a skein of wool under the bed near its saucer of milk. There were the lifting and rending noises of men at work. The rookery was quiet. He snapped to attention when he saw them.

"Ah, Mukund...back. Good. How are you?"

"First class, huzoor."

He was still saluting with a smile as the trees crashed down one by one.

FIFTEEN SKETCHES OF RUMI

I have these dreams.

Selma is massaging Ammi's legs and arms. With a start, she realizes that she has begun to strangle her. She knows as she is doing this that she has dozed off during the massage and has dreamed the whole sequence. I am imagining this although I wake up in the dream before she does. I don't remember at what point I actually wake up or how it ends.

I am sitting in the cane chair in the verandah across from Papa, who is reading the newspaper. I slowly lift the empty twelve bore, crook it against my shoulder, and, sighting down the barrels, draw a bead dead centre on his forehead. At the last minute, I jerk it away and aim at a bird—a bulbul?—singing in the bel tree. To my surprise, there's an explosion. Feathers and leaves drift down. I wake up every time, feeling clammy and panicked. I dream of this often, and every time my body reacts as if it were real, more real than reality.

Yesterday, I began a letter to Rumi Bhai. Suddenly, I realized it was too late. He had gone. Some years ago.

I seek refuge in repetition and routine: the blinking red lights, the footfall of silence in the hall, the drip in the arm. The crackle of numbers over the intercom like a priest reciting at some ancient mystery lends sleep over the talk of the automatic clock. Sometimes.

I think I did this in charcoal. A few tucks of the motor dying to a cough as if throttled. His Vespa has entered the front yard. I hear the click as Khalifa, our cook, lifts the latch.

"And where is my learned friend? At the courts passing judgment on some groundling?" Rumi Bhai asks as he locks his scooter and pockets the key.

"Your MLF is at the Government Press ground," Selma says.

"It's the semis. We're playing Railways. You promised Ammi. You said you'd take us to the match after school, remember?" I remind him.

"Did you bring me a chocolate? Rumi Bhai, you promised," Selma asks.

Our satchels are on the sofa. I could say that our school pinafores are blue and his tweed jacket green, the sweater yellow, but the colours have bled out of the picture, if they were there at all. I have drawn his head squarer than it was. His leg looks oddly stumpy. Was I trying my hand at foreshortening?

"Did you bring me a chocolate?" he imitates the whine. "I promised nothing of the kind. Chocs for you horrors, you spoiled sisters? Lahol bilaquwat. What about your teeth? They will rot. Go and get ready quickly."

Suddenly, the chocolate bars are conjured aloft from the sleeve where they had been wrapped in a silk handkerchief. All along.

There are whoops of joy as we leap to claim the prizes and escape to the kitchen, shouting, "Khalifa, we'll help."

By the time we emerge with a clatter of cups, having whisked the coffee, cream, and sugar into a paste, he has settled in front of the Japanese silkscreen painting. He keeps studying the figure with the parasol under the cherry blossom tree intently. He then flips through my sketchbook, pausing at the crayon drawings of roses and dahlias. Vivek, a boy, brings in a plate of biscuits and savouries. Khalifa pours the hot water and milk for the coffee as Munna, her son, and Vivek serve. Selma wipes the wisp of caramel on her lip with her finger before taking a rusk.

Rumi Bhai eases back into the sofa. From his right-hand jacket pocket comes the paperback, which he places on the table.

"How odd of God…" he recites solemnly, his moustache wet with foam, a chocolate crisp in his saucer, the little finger of his right hand crooked daintily away from the cup.

I sit and sketch.

※

I am snuggled against Ammi in the green room facing the verandah. Her hair, which reaches her waist, smells of patchouli. Selma and Khalifa are sitting across her shelling peas into a blue plastic basin.

Hunza Apa is visiting from Phaphamau. She is sitting on her haunches and talking to Ammi about a proposal they have received for Razia, her granddaughter.

"The boy is a gaddi from Kesariya but they have money. The other son is a doctor. He's in America."

"You know, Hunza, I don't care about such things. Gaddi, waddi. It doesn't make a difference. As long as he's decent and the family isn't dishonest, that's all that matters. It's time we shed all this caste and sect and other nonsense."

I hug Ammi harder.

Even in this light, I can see that I have sketched five figures in the hush of twilight. I am on the ground, my face propped on an elbow, the free hand tracing the mosaic on the floor. The verandah is tiled with pieces of china from old tea sets. Selma and I are trying to find the rest of the green Spode dragon on the floor in the gloom. When I turn to my left, I can see into Rumi Bhai's drawing room. The samovar has a gleam. If I squint hard enough, I can discern the painting on the mantelpiece: the rajah in jewels, elephants, howdahs, horses, archers, deer, and servitors. To my right, there is a gas lantern. Its sock-bulb is hissing, and mosquitoes are buzzing and bumping into it with anger.

There are shadows. One is that of the light switch on the wall that falls across us like the dome of a mosque. Another attaches to his father, who is sitting in a wicker chair. He is holding a book upside down. (Later, I learned this was his Göttingen festschrift on Vulgar Latin philology.) He is covered with a white soutane, and his hair and beard are snowy. In a corner, Rumi Bhai and Ammi and Papa are talking about money and servants and the old days. Our host is wrapped in a pashmina shawl. I remember one story:

"The Nizam of Hyderabad was such a miser. He had rooms full of bullion and jewels and paper money that just rotted away. Once, when the viceroy was visiting for dinner, we were all served on gold plates. It was very formal. Protocol and precedence demanded that no one touch the food before the Nizam. Of course, the Nizam being the fellow that he was would take two quick bites from each course and stop before the diners had even started. By the time they had raised their spoons, the servants had cleared the table. When the final course was placed before the Nizam, he exclaimed 'Ah, but the halva is indigestible today.' It was whisked away before anyone had a chance to touch it. All the guests, including the viceroy, went home hungry from the table of the world's richest man."

He holds a pipe, or does he? Is it a cigar? Did he smoke cigars? I don't remember.

Selma skips down to the porch near the garden wall. She is holding something. What is it? As she opens her fist, I spy a tiny, oblong sac with black threads. It is pulsing with light. A firefly. Our breaths stop. Our movements are slow, stilled, and gentle. We have changed in that instant. The light-bearer lies there for a moment, winking before it flies away. Soon we will have to go in. We will be told that we will catch colds lying on the floor and that our sweaters will get dirty and that there is school tomorrow so get ready to go. It is that time.

※

I can feel the rub of the canvas of this day under my fingertips. The sky is shot with cobalt. A Sickertian blue, a Cimabuen blue, a Minoan blue. A spotless sky. Even today, I can run my fingers over that sky and feel its colours scraped on *impasti* with my palate knife. A sky that lives and lisps on cloth. I am on his north verandah again but in my bare feet. The mosaic is cool. In the distance, nearly where this sky ends, I can see the thin brown arm of the river hugging the mustard fields, which are topped with yellow. The banks are large with rain. There is nothing of the clayey smear of an Amrita Sher Gill in this composition. The morning haze has burned off.

I sense the soutane beside me.

"There was a Greek who marched for months with his men and stood unbelieving with relief before the Black Sea." I see a caret here. Did he really say "unbelieving with relief" or did Selma add it here later? I can't be sure.

I do not tell him that I am trying to see thin brown forms in white lay marigolds at the shrine, which is topped with a saffron flag, although none of this is visible.

"Did he shout '*Eureka*'?" Pause. "Archimedes?"

A thin smile. Gentle. "No, quite another Greek," he says as he grips my hand and we descend into the basement to the library. His hand is warm and soft.

I have that copy of *Anabasis* at home.

⁂

We are back in our drawing room. Earlier or later than that canvas, I can't say. Rumi Bhai is berating Dr. Ganguly on the practice of oiling hair.

"All you need is a good champi with water. Nothing of this disgusting grease under one's hat. Most unsanitary. A magnet for dirt and midges. Maybe we should ask Ashfaq here to speak to Mr. Butt at the city to ban it."

He pronounces it "greeze." We are amused. Dr. Ganguly has taken off his lambswool hat uncomfortably to reveal a well-oiled tonsure. (For years afterwards, Selma called it his "halo.")

"I fear we are boring our learned friend," Rumi Bhai declares.

Papa stops snoring.

"I'll always remember the night you shot a black panther, Ashfaq, from a distance. What was it, two hundred yards? A nine-and-a-half-footer. It had made the mistake, Ganguly Sahib, of peering out from behind a tree. All one could see were its eyes. But what eyes. They gleamed like coals at night, live coals. A superb shot. The best I've seen."

"It had killed three children in the tarai area and had moved near to the hills of Agra. Can you imagine? In those days, we did not have telescopic sights and whatnot. Just my Jeffery twelve bore. A good gun." Papa looks animated, Dr. Ganguly appeased.

"The shot passed clean through the eye socket and the brain, did it not?" Rumi Bhai asks.

Papa is now telling everyone about how he once shot two charazes and invited the conservationist who told him not to to dinner.

"There are only four left now. Ah, but who could resist the taste of saffron in that flesh? He ate well, I tell you. It's a different world now. You can't even hunt a lizard," Papa says to his guests.

Dr. Ganguly, a devout vegetarian, looks aghast. Then it is a discussion of hunting scenes in poetry. Dr. Ganguly, who teaches Urdu at the university, talks about the depictions of the simurgh. The head of a dog, the tail of a peacock, a lion's claws, four wings, orange feathers, and a silver-capped head. Was it a roc, a bustard, a florican, a bird of paradise, an ortolan, or a hoopoe? I remember a pipe or a cigar being waved (whose?), voices raised, and the chink of the silver teapot on the glass top.

Later, Selma asks Papa what Rumi Bhai was like at the university. Was he always fond of plants and flowers? Did he play cricket then?

"He was senior to me. His father taught me ancient languages." There is an elliptical finality to that. The last brush stroke.

HAPPINESS and other DISORDERS

The units of installation that make up Raheela Ashfaq's Papilionidae series are better described as stations, in the religio-iconographical sense, in the life of the "family," constructed as a narrative of personal and artistic struggle. The compositions are simple enough to be random. Butterflies, pupae, caterpillars, and chrysalises are mounted on cork. Some are backed on stencilled plywood, on cardboard, on canvases, or on drawing and photographic paper that has been exposed, creating a palimpsest of the world of artifice contesting with nature morte. Objects—created, discovered, dead, preserved, accidental, or willed—are overlaid, often alongside, in arrangements of textures and significations that disrupt time and pose corrosive challenges to perspective and interpretation of what is presented and re-presented as history is dismembered and re-membered...

Selma is crying. I can feel her tears track hotly down the cheeks. The traces of her tears look like plough marks. She is fighting Ammi who holds her tight between her knees. Ammi's mouth is full of pins, and her fingers are cat's cradles of rubber bands. She is twisting and braiding Selma's hair. I can feel my sister's skin tighten at the temple. It will be my turn next. I start wailing. Ammi tells Khalifa to bring the bangles that she bought yesterday from chowk.

"These girls. Be still or your pinafore will get ruined. Miss Seraphica won't want such a dirty girl in her class. See, aren't they beautiful? For my little Simmo."

The bangles are thin, glass: green and red. The pins and rubber bands snap into place. Selma crawls off the takhat sniffing, her eyes rheumy with hurt, clutching her yellow canvas satchel and the bangles. I am dragged howling into position next.

Sometimes there's a day trip to the dairy where Rumi Bhai works. We go in our green Ambassador with its listing axle. It's "bags I the window seat" and "shifto" as we jostle for seats. The car groans as Munawwar changes gears. Whenever we turn a corner, Ammi pushes Selma away with an "uff" when she falls against her. I remember rolling down the window and feeling the soft puff of wind kiss my face and hair, and drawing Selma close to me as we sing or hum whatever comes into our heads: "Wee Willie Winkie" or

> *One fine morning, in the middle of the night,*
> *two dead dogs began to fight.*
> *A deaf, dumb, and blind man passing by*
> *heard them fight and began to cry.*

We would cross the bridge over the sandy flats and look down to see people washing clothes in the river. Once we blew a tire on the bridge, and the driver changed it while a train passed overhead. The struts and rivets of the bridge rattled, which made us squeal and cling to each other. We could see the train and the clouds scudding in the reflection in the river.

Once we reached the dairy, a peon would meet us. In my mind's eye, Rumi Bhai then comes bouncing out of his office, puts on a smock, and troops us into the dairy where we watch the cows being milked—if we are on time—as they shift in their beds of hay. The cows look at us with long eyelashes fringing their soft brown eyes. We try to pet the calves in the pen. Selma almost fell over the paling once. It took a milkshake to quieten her. There is this sharp animal smell of urine, dung, raw milk, and of disinfectant. In the next scene, the four of us are seated on the lawn under the gulmohar blooms as the ice cream arrives in paper tubs with wooden paddlets for spoons. The chairs are made of bamboo. My scarf almost always catches on a nail. This is a summer scene.

We are in Agra. I am worried about Selma who has just had an attack of bronchitis. She must be six or seven. Her atomizer with its pink rubber bulb is lying beside her. She is still wheezing as she writes in her exercise book. Later, I am standing in the backyard near the cook's quarters. Noor is holding a rooster by its legs. It has metallic red, green, and brown feathers. Its wattles wag as it struggles from time to time. He mutters the formula while he lowers the bird to the ground. He holds a knife in his other hand, which he then draws slowly across the feathery throat. Blood is scattering on the dust like rubies. The cock has started its dance of death. A set of ungainly flops as it moves to an unknowable beat. Selma is shrieking. Her tears mingle with snot. Selma begins to hit him, her tiny fists balled with anger.

"Noor, I will put you in jail. Ammi, call the police."

"Ji, begumsahib. Here I am. Arrest me," says Noor, proffering his hands for handcuffs, careful to angle the knife away from Selma. I notice that the wooden handle of the knife is missing.

Later, she stands red-eyed, heaving but quiet outside the cook's hut, her hand in Noor's who recites the cooking instructions through his betel-stained teeth. There is a heap of feathers, and offal for the cat.

Do I have the light right? It's almost May, the day after my twelfth birthday. We are playing cricket. Vivek has drawn stumps on the wall with yellow chalk: three shaky lines that reach my armpit. I am batting. Vivek bowls a fast one, and I miss it.

"Out," screams Selma.

Vivek: "Out, clean bowled, yes."

"Not out. Trial ball," I scream, but my new Harrow No. 5 bat is dragged away from my grip. Helpless, I beat my fists on Vivek's chest. He stands quietly with the bat. I push him to the ground and fall on him, crying and punching. He is surprised but doesn't resist. I feel a rough hand pulling me up. It is Papa. I have drawn hatchmarks on his forehead, but his face was probably puffy the way it used to get when he became angry.

"How many times have I told you not to play with servants? Don't you ever listen?"

I am dragged inside. The leather sandal knocks me sideways, and I cry even louder.

"Not on her face, jaani, not on her face." Ammi's voice comes, approving and advising, but it's too late. Papa is unbuckling his belt.

"No, jaani, that is enough. Raheela, promise Papa you will not fight with that boy. Stop crying. You are lucky. Do you know what my khalamma used to do to the servant girls who annoyed her? She would hang them upside down from the hooks. Do you see them? Look up, there, yes those, and whip them till their kurtas were sticky with blood."

Ammi pinches my thigh hard when I begin to bawl. They murmur about paying "that boy's family" to move to Sassurkhaderi.

"I will marry him," my voice rising in defiance between sobs.

"Marry him? Whom? I will give you 'marry.'" A second slap. "Who would marry you, except a servant? Black like a Madrasi."

"Get out, you rotten child. Playing cricket and drawing. At your age. Always with a bat and always drawing, What good is that? Why can't you be like Selma and learn to write or something? She wins all these prizes. Look at you," Ammi says, with a touch of exasperation in her voice.

I know I will not go to school the next day. This one has left an imprint of everything, even the ring, on my cheek. It burns when I cry.

Ms. Ashfaq's exhibition frontispiece is the Papilionidae series: swallowtails pinned and shiny; the common mormon, the common jay, the lime butterfly, the common rose, the crimson rose, all of whose wings have been overpainted with abstract shapes in all the four stages of life. Male casuarina flowers with bracteoles are stuffed into the margins of the red box frames. Inserted are transcriptions, sometimes in a child's cursive, of war diaries from different sources: Persian, Greek, Japanese, and English, and some family postcards...

Later the same day: I am in my pinafore in a rickshaw with a suitcase and my sketchbook in my school bag. He is before me at the gate. My head is bowed. He does not look surprised.

"Dinesh, pay the rickshaw wallah and then prepare the blue room. Give the suitcase to Bilquis. The begumsahib will be staying for a few days. And bring some tea," Rumi Bhai tells his servant.

A plate of chumchums, sandesh, éclairs, and profiteroles appears. He leans forward as he listens gravely. He clicks his teeth once or twice. A hanky is pulled from his sleeve when my tears come.

"Let me not to the marriage of true minds admit impediment," he intones, offering it.

In my sketch, the bed is rigged with canvas straps woven crossly. A steel almirah is in the corner. My school bag is on the top of the teak dresser, my suitcase beside it. The fan is moving slowly overhead. I have been asleep. I become aware of voices. I tilt my head back from the pillow. Above, there is a bookshelf with some paperbacks. The walls are blue with distemper. In another ward and in another time, I'd have recognized the scent of soap and colour in this freshly painted room as a hospital smell. The right side of my face is almost blue.

I put on my sandals and head away from the sounds to the garden by the west wall. There is a breeze strong enough to lift my curls. It is darker than I thought. Jasmine blossoms are unfolding, their reek heavy and oppressive. With it mingles the tang of clementines, which hang like nuggets of gold under the shadow of the leaves. There are still a few butterflies, bees, and hornets near the hollyhocks. Past the flame of the forest that has shed some red on the floor, there is a lemon grove. I walk looking out for fallen fruit or stumps. I am wary of snakes and of twisting my ankle.

I have reached the rose garden. Some of the grafts are tied with string. They are all twisted like old dancers gnarled into different attitudes. The whooping evensong of the chakki where the boatfolk take their grain to be milled is getting louder. Dinesh is using a mattock to quarry the water into a vegetable patch. He looks up and smiles. The tube well is strumming under the old acacia tree with its long thorns. The mustard fields have disappeared in the gloom. Lights appear near the shore. I spend an hour wandering in the orchard and chasing butterflies.

I come upon them later on the north verandah: six lawyers, including a woman, in their gowns and bibs. To the side stands Justice Pandey with his wife. Mr. Karolia from the big grey house across the street, Ahmed Billa, Sultan Amin, and Hashim Siddiqui in his police inspector's uniform are in the circle. It is easy to spot Dr. Ganguly's lambswool. His son Suresh is with him, a tall, surly boy with wild eyes who laughs when you talk to him. (Papa likes him. He calls him "the son I never had." He's always in our house snickering with Munna, the cook's son.) I can see some men in dhotis and sadhus in saffron walking with Dinesh to the gate. There are four cars, a jeep, and a scooter in the driveway.

"Every year, our P.N. Oakes find these sacred hidden underground rivers and these heads."

"Dinesh, get three seers of ladoos from Pandit Malluram's shop tomorrow morning. Give them to the pandit as an offering. Tell him that I'll send some money later to place before Saraswatiji whose bust they found near the shrine."

"These aren't pandits. Troublemakers. Bad sadhus, very bad. Thugs, some of them. You get them at the mela."

"Did you hear that? I'll bet you the bust'll be plaster of Paris. Not even stone."

"Ah, our sleeping beauty...Raheela, Ashfaq Sahib's eldest, you know. Here, for a short holiday."

"Easement, indeed. A ploy. What comes next, Rumi Sahib? The run of the house?"

"But we must respect this, of course."

"Maybe but you must also act quickly. Maybe Ishwar Sarai Sahib at the courts. I'll talk to him if I see him at the Willingdon Club tonight."

"Raheela, you must come to see us. Suman will be so happy to have you over," Mrs. Pandey says to me.

But now they are talking about Diwali celebrations and then those interminable judicial stories. I only remember a fragment from Justice Pandey's account of a theft from a Christian bakery.

"But, m'lud, this was no heinous crime. Just a chocolate torte." Laughter.

The tea things are taken in. Mr. Billa's black Hillman is the first to move out of the porch. That was a cicada, I think, that whirred past my face.

⁂

An hour later, the gong goes for dinner. It is a quiet affair. His father sits, all in white, at the head of the table. A small Aga cooker is placed beside him. I am seated to his left. Bilquis, his cook, who is even more bent in this picture than I recall, whisks in butter, cream, flour, and salt over the cooker and pours it over the cauliflowers. His father insists on serving me first. It is delicious. Rumi Bhai is pensive at the foot of the table, chewing the end of his moustache and making clicking sounds. Later, we have carp with mustard seeds on rice, Bengali style, and a syllabub, or was it a soufflé, with tea. After a while, Rumi Bhai reads aloud a passage from Winwood Reade on how the prophet's fits were epileptic, not revelatory. It is a night without dreams.

Breakfast. The cooker is on the verandah this time. Bilquis is making an omelette. There is fresh cream sprinkled with icing sugar in a bowl. Blood oranges gape on my plate. I tear open a croissant, so hot that it scalds my fingers, and I put them in my mouth and suck them slowly. Rumi Bhai returns with a bowl full of pomegranates, grapefruit, aamlas, guavas, mangoes, and clementines, which he places in the centre of the glass table. "My homegrown epergne. For my guest." I am still not sure what an epergne is or where his father was. I had spent that afternoon on the verandah, sketching the garden and the fields leading to the river.

I hear the familiar gear and flee to the blue room. I can now identify the voices: Papa's bass, Selma's sing-song skimming over the others like a dragonfly flying low before the rains, Ammi's snorting laugh. Soon, Bilquis and Dinesh are pleading with me. Selma appears but I take her hand and usher her into the library. "Don't touch anything." It is wonderful and musty and full of books. I think about how marvellous it would be to read a book in another language. Like watching a blank piece of photographic paper come to life with shapes in the red light of a darkroom. She reads a translation of Claudian while I pick up a book on butterflies of Asia.

We go up into the drawing room, and I start reading a paperback. It is *The Arrangement*, I remember. Papa enters with a smile, humouring me with entreaties, caresses, and hugs. Ammi embraces me, cries a little, and pops a rasgulla into my mouth.

"I have a box of these from Malluram's for you at home."

"I don't want them. I don't like them. I like Lucky's."

"But you always did when you were younger. Malluram's rasgullas were your favourites. Accha, tell me, where did you get this starch, grumpy? Nobody else in this family has it. Let's go home. Come on, Raheela darling." Laughing.

"I don't want to go. I am happy here."

"You have school tomorrow," Papa says.

I see Munawwar and Dinesh hauling my suitcase and school bag to the car. The betrayal is complete.

"Khalifa's made those special kawabs that you like," Ammi adds.

I am resigned and return to the book in the drawing room. The air has eased, and they have started talking. I emerge on the verandah with the book.

"Please, Papa, what is 'phallus'?" I ask loudly. Pause. "It's in the book." A longer pause in the discussion and then it resumes, overeager.

I ask about Vivek. Again, the silence. I don't care to remember the journey home.

꽃

My method: *You will need gin or vodka and a small dish. Pour some over the paper in the dish. Use stamp tongs to take the dried specimen from the bag, and place it on the paper. Or add some gin to the thorax with a dropper. I like uncurling the proboscis if I can by first using a syringe and tongs. After fifteen minutes, I try moving the wings to see if they are relaxed enough and then I mount it with brightly coloured ento pins on to drawing paper or on to canvas, which is trickier. Did I miss the glassine?*

꽃

Ammi asks me what I think of her mother. "Isn't she beautiful?" I don't say anything as expected about Nani's fair skin or grey eyes, or even her moustache.

"I think she's fat."

Ammi laughs and says Nani loves her lovely dark granddaughter. Didn't I like the Winsor & Newton paint set she had brought for me? I am her favourite. She is visiting from England, which she keeps mentioning as if it was something we lacked. Nani looks like a cat and is just as strange. I don't like her much but I don't tell Ammi this.

We are all sitting on the verandah with towels over our heads, peering into buckets. It's a lunar eclipse. After it passes, Nani says, "How can they send men up there? It is ridiculous. All lies." She keeps asking us when we will get married. Selma likes being petted on the head. She says Nani smells of roses.

Mimi, Noori Khala's daughter, is travelling with Nani. Noori Khala is Ammi's younger sister. Nani tells us that because Ruksana Khala, Ammi's youngest sister, had married a red-faced man from Wapping, our other cousin, Pammi, is spotted. "Brown and pink spots. That's what happens when you mix colours, you see." Selma and I believed this for quite a while until we saw the photographs of Pammi with her parents.

Mimi is fourteen and leads us on walks and says odd things like "wotcher" and what sounds like "innit" and other words that she gobbles up. Rumi Bhai chuckles and teases her gently when she speaks.

"We had a flat in Didcot."

"Weren't you carrying a stepney then?" Rumi Bhai asks.

"A what?"

"A spare tire. God, you English." Annoyed because his joke is spoiled.

Mimi is tall, with green eyes. She has a pigeon-toed way of walking, of strutting forward while her head and shoulders wobble with each stride. She finds strange things. Her ponytail waves every time she stoops for a piece of driftwood from the shore, seashells, fallen leaves, and stones that we have to carry for her. Once, she brings home a puppy, which she names "Enoch Powell" or "EP."

EP is black with russet-tipped ears and a tail so curly that it touches its back. It follows her everywhere, but Papa is firm about not allowing it in the house. Mimi gives it milk and bread in a plate on the verandah, but EP takes to eating dirt and pebbles once she forgets about it. Most days, it deposits these cairns of small stones every few feet on the black and white flagstones like pawns on a chessboard. Twice, Selma and I come upon Munna beating it with a ruler. We're not sure if he will stop as we have told him to.

One evening, I remember, we found EP in the driveway in a pool of blood. Its head was smashed. I remember being surprised that its tail was still curled. It was as if I expected that death would straighten it. What else do I recall? Selma and I with Nani's black burkhas draped over our shoulders, candles in our hands, heads bent over a hole beneath the bel tree where Mimi buries EP in a shoebox. She folds her hands and incantates solemn nothings. Papa had the area sprayed after the flies appeared.

Selma was sent home from school, Ammi tells me. Her chemistry teacher, Mr. Sarkar, had marched her to the principal's office. He had overheard her calling him "The Great Litmus."

"Well, he always wears blue and goes red whenever we mention love" is what she tells me brightly, her head nodding, "and I love reading Byron and Ghalib aloud."

There are other reports from Miss Seraphica, the headmistress. Simmo seems to read romances and poetry all the time, and skips classes to go to the cinema with Meenakshi and Nilufer and her brother, Rohinton. Aside from English, her school work is poor. Papa is concerned.

Soon, the suitors start arriving. One is a dentist with a cast in his eye and a stammer. Selma and I are never sure if he's addressing Ammi or Papa when he talks. Selma mimics him mercilessly for days.

"You know, t-t-t-t-there is a new t-t-t-t-technique for b-b-b-b-bic-c-c-cuspids."

Wait, wasn't there also a distant cousin, a gold medallist, who was thinking of migrating to Australia to become a plastic surgeon? Yes, that strange Salman who had kept winking at us. We'd dash off into the bedroom, our hands over our mouths, convulsed with giggles. There were others. They were not important.

I remember the day it happened. Ammi has given me the folded umbrella to shake out as she comes in from the rain. The ferrule is clammy. She is smiling.

"Raheela, it's agreed. Selma has accepted Zahoor."

"Zahoor? Who is Zahoor?" My mind is a blank.

"Zahoor, your Mehbooba Khala's son." Like vitriol dribbled on canvas.

A feeling like straining after the last fading notes of the gong. My teeth and fist are clenched, but I do not let anything show.

"But he's...so old."

"Accha, accha, but Selma likes him. It's decided. Oh, Rumi Bhai's father is very ill. We must go."

I ask Selma. She doesn't really mind him at all even if his face looks like a crushed bun with currants for eyes. He is kind, she says.

The tracery of henna and the clinking of bangles is still with me. Razia is drawing Selma's hair through a jewelled ivory comb that is loaded with scented oil. Nilufer, Suman, and Meenakshi are threading jasmine in a blue basin for hair garlands. Hunza Apa and Ammi are applying the henna. Selma is beautiful. I dab her eyes with a hanky to stop the kohl running. There is a figure at the door in the sketch whom I can't identify. I know it can't be Suresh, who is off somewhere supervising the food and the tent arrangements. Munna is looking after the band members and the lighting. It isn't Papa. He is with the lawyers, in-laws, and the mullah. I am preparing the bridal suite for the night.

"No men, no men," the women start chanting. Rumi Bhai ignores them. He is in a black achkan.

"For my wonderful child," he says, pressing a kiss on Selma's forehead and placing an envelope in her lap. She clings to him. He goes quickly. Selma is crying again. The teasing has started.

"Has Selma stopped praying?"

"Her prayers will be answered. She'll have seven children."

"Don't fret, Selma darling. Your groom's coming on a black horse."

Clapping and songs and laughter.

Inside the marquee, the sunlight is dappled as it strains through the red-and-blue appliqué designs. The guests are arriving. Papa and I greet them. Ammi is still with Selma. Shehnaz Auntie wears a banarsi silk sari and a pearl choker. She looks lovely. Mrs. Haider and Mrs. Hidayatullah want to see the bride. As I escort them, I notice the Gangulys talking to Mr. Hidayatullah and his sons, Tariq and Khalid, in a group that includes Mr. Billa and the Broomes. There may have been others. The Dhillons from Lakhimpur. Yes, Mehbooba Khala had patted my head and asked when I would be next.

Rumi Bhai appears by my side when I return.

"Ah, there's old 'But Because Maudwell.'"

"Why do you call him that?" I ask.

"The name's stuck since school. I've listened to him often enough. It's always 'not because' of something or the other 'but because.'"

The Karolias have seen him. Mrs. K. is fluttering her eyelashes crusted with mascara. They make straight for us.

"Aha, Rumi Sahib, I was just telling Jenny, the days of the chronic bachelor are over, don't you think? It's time we got you hitched. Jenny has found a wonderful match. You know the Khabeesullah's daughter?" says Mr. Karolia.

"Do you mean Rehana, the journalist in Delhi? The one whose teeth go out for a walk?" Rumi Bhai asks.

"Poor Raheela, you must be so sad. Your only sister, ey, sweetheart?" Mrs. Karolia says to me.

"Ah, you know what they say. Even Quickfix can't mend broken hearts," Mr. Karolia gives up with a laugh. They move towards the Guptas, Samiullahs, and Sarkars, who have arrived as a group.

"Meddling fool. Uses rapeseed oil instead of butter. Mr. and Mrs. Tastee Biscuits, indeed." Rumi Bhai sucks on his teeth as he delivers this verdict.

Then, just as quickly, he turns twinkingly humorous.

"I think everyone should get married at least twice. Once to acquire immunity; the other times to test it. Who needs that fatty degeneration of the moral spirit? Just don't tell Selma that. RLS knew," he says, smiling a little.

Rumi Bhai has joined Mr. Maudwell, Justice Pandey, and Dr. Ganguly, some lawyers and cricketers. Someone tells a joke about an Afghan spotting a peach across the river, which I don't understand. I am shooed away when I ask for an explanation. "Not for the ears of young ladies." When I leave I hear something about "Ovaltine.... Ah yes, isn't that what women do once a month?" Snuffling laughter follows.

Miss Seraphica has arrived with flowers. I rush to find a vase. I am very tired. The rest is a tableau of noise, tannoys, voices, singing, bunting, caresses, tears, jokes, laughter, presents, and food, lots of food. I have tried to sketch some of it from photos, but everything looks unreal and remote.

I remember Selma at the car window, clinging to my hand, crying. Zahoor Bhai presses my hand. Ammi leans into the car and hugs Selma, while Papa stands behind tearfully. The house felt hollow for months afterwards.

❦

Artist's statement: *As the Estremadurans scythed their way from Villahermosa to Peru, they left behind blood, fear, and faith. In the name of their quadrafoiled God, the priests claimed the massacres were in fact and in spirit liberations of the unblessed. A strange legacy ensued. Believing this to be the Christian way, Mayan leaders began crucifying their human sacrifices to the powers who allowed the world to be born again every day. Of course, this has nothing to do with the pre-Columbian crosses that even today pick out the hills of Chiapas like telegraph poles...*

❦

Disguises, lures, and transmutations had obviously fascinated me in my final year of school at St. Sophia's. Was I that intrigued by how one element changes into another? The chapter on nuclear physics in my Newton and Abbott is scored with red pencil. Page after page in my sketchbook has drawings of glow-worms, butterflies, and geckoes, and their tails that keep twitching even after they have dropped off. (Selma would use a twig, my bat, or even an awl to get the lizards to run away, leaving their tails behind.) The exercise books that I have still are full of equations on chemiluminescence in fireflies. I recall I used to sit by the orchard wall for hours studying blues, mantises, snakeskins, chrysalises, and rose grafts, or whatever hooked my interest. There are some coloured-chalk copies from books of predators that merge with their surroundings. This was the year that I was accepted at Kanpur University. I had decided to study zoology. Ammi was relieved but Papa asked, "Can Sohaila look after her? After all, she's old." "But, jaani, Raheela is old enough to take care of her. And Kanpur is only an hour or so away." I don't recall thinking about studying art at all.

In this, Selma looks older and heavier. We are in the green room at the back of our house. Through the meshes we can see the heat shimmer off the flagstones in the verandah, although it is only ten in the morning. The fan is going at top speed. Selma is telling Khalifa something. I think I have drawn her two daughters standing to the right, but I suspect I am wrong. Wasn't one of Zahra or Asma in Aligarh then? Zahoor Bhai is seated, one leg tucked under the other, on the takhat talking to Ammi about mangoes. Does Rumi Bhai's hunch look exaggerated in this? His hair is thinner in the sketch but that is barely an outline. He was definitely frailer. Yes, he coughed persistently. Papa seemed irritated by that.

Rumi Bhai is talking to Suresh who is playing chess with Hanif Chacha, Papa's elder brother, who is visiting from Roorkee. Munna and Papa are watching intently but the game is at a standstill.

"And just what exactly do you and your friends know about Nehru? He was part of the elite. True. English-educated. Yes. He was. But just look at your politicians. What are they? Criminals. Murderers. Illiterates, most of them. Raving about mandirs and masjids. Just because they put on homespun doesn't make them workers. Most wouldn't sit near a peasant or touch a lower caste. Thrice horrible. I'll tell you what they are. They are cat poo," Rumi Bhai says.

Suresh cackles at this heat.

It could have been the same Saturday afternoon. There is the earthy smell and chill from the desert fan. Selma is wearing a sweater ("my bronchitis"). All the doors and windows have been bolted. The light enters the dining room through the green bubbled-glass panes and skylights. Pages of *The Northern India Patrika* are spread on the floor. In the middle of this is a metal bucket filled with cold water and mangoes. Everyone is seated cross-legged, picking out dassehris and langdas, kneading, biting, and sucking. Squelching noises and dribbles of juice emerge from every mouth. The pile of skins and seeds is growing quickest in front of Hanif Chacha. We devour three bucketfuls before Zahoor Bhai produces a case of alphonsos. Then we stagger off to wash and nap.

The boundaries of the courts' cricket ground have been freshly painted. All around the oval are tiny flags in pink, yellow, red, and blue. The field is brown and scurfy. The ground is packed with spectators. Papa's team is fielding. I am back for the winter holidays. I feel hot and red and like shrinking every time Papa struggles to pick up the ball or run. The cantonment supporters are vocal.

"Please put some servants to field for the Commissioner Sahib. It's too hot."

"Arrey, Ashfaq Sahib, Captain Sahib, the biryani must have been delicious last night."

"Or was it the murgh musallum? Our compliments to the chef."

Scooters' treble horns are tweaked whenever a boundary is hit.

"Well hit, sir. Our own black Dexter."

"We want sixers."

"Abey, Rastogi, bowl on the off stump. You'll hit the umpire if you carry on like this."

Rumi Bhai, frail ("his father's death, the poor man," murmurs Mrs. Pandey), Sultan Amin, and Justice Pandey are munching peanuts and following the match. Ammi and Mrs. Pandey are talking as they supervise the food.

"Suman couldn't come, Raheela. She's at a friend's studying for an exam."

There is a mark on Rumi Bhai's neck. I notice the mottled, wine-coloured streak when the ascot moves as he eats.

Piyush is batting. Papa gets him lbw for 61. The applause sounds like a matchbox being shaken.

"Who got out?"

"Piyush. Vivek's brother."

"Clever boys. I hear Vivek's studying engineering," says Rumi Bhai slowly.

Ammi shoots him a warning glance.

"Probably through the reservation quota," Mrs. Pandey opines. "No place for real merit students these days. Look at Trilok, my sister's boy. Topper but can't get a seat in IIT. All given over to these boys."

※

I spot Dinesh first. He is walking past the large pots of biryani, plates of kawabs, and naans. He is wearing a shawl. His hair is completely white in contrast with his almost blue skin. He looks like a photographic negative. He crooks a finger at Rumi Bhai, who gets up and murmurs something to us before walking off to his car.

Justice Pandey and Sultan Amin exchange looks.

"Ammi, does Dinesh wear Rumi Bhai's shawl and drive his scooter all the time now? Is Rumi Bhai ill?" I ask.

Ammi's mouth is set in a hard line. Her grip tightens on my hand.

"He's not well. The shawl was probably old. I expect Rumi Bhai gave it to him. Can you ask the cook to start the tea, jaani? The players will be coming in after eight overs."

The big silver cups line the cupboard in the drawing room. I think Papa's team won the match and the league that year.

※

I have seen many crucifixions. This is mine:

I am struggling as I lie on the takhat in the green room. Suresh and Selma are gripping my hands apart. I feel I am being torn in two. Khalifa is crying, "Please, please."

My eyes are stinging and swollen. When I open them, I see Ammi sitting on my legs, one hand pressing my belly down and the other tipping the contents of a canister over my kameez. It is pungent and slippery with a cockroachy smell. Papa is pushing an oily rag into my mouth. I am thrashing my head from side to side. I resist but he forces it open. I gag, arching my back. I see a crowd gripping the mesh and peering in, saying nothing, just looking.

"Munna, some matches from the kitchen. Now. Hanif Bhai, get me the gun."

❧

Despite myself, I am laughing. He looks ridiculous in that wig. His lipstick has smudged. The moustache is gone. His finger is at his lip.

"Dinesh has gone to see his son. We have just a little time."

Why is Rumi Bhai dressed in a shalwar kameez and why the rouge? Nothing makes sense. I am near tears, gripping the doorpost.

He holds out a shirt, a tweed jacket, a sweater, trousers, and shoes.

"Here are the keys. But first change into these. I think they'll fit."

He notes the hesitation.

"They're watching from the bridge. I'm going ahead on the scooter. If they see me from that distance, maybe they'll think it's you. It'll draw them off. Go straight to the station. I have booked a second-class ticket for you on the Kalka

Mail in my name. It goes in an hour. You can take the car ten minutes after I have gone. Once you get there, stay in the toilet until the train leaves."

His tone is urgent now.

"But I'm not sure about the shoes. Raheela, listen to me. Do as I say. There's no time to be lost. Here, take these too," he says, thrusting a sheaf of papers at me.

"What are they?"

"My Tastee Biscuits shares."

"No, I can't." I am close to wailing.

"Silly girl. Take them. Here are five thousand rupees. I will wire you more in Delhi. My aunt's driver will pick you up. I have explained everything to her. Nuzhat Mumani has already notified Vivek."

Vivek. All my confusion and indecision disappear. I take everything he gives me except the shares. I hand them back. He hugs me hard. I know when he turns that he is crying, but I rush inside. My suitcase is ready.

❦

How did it all happen? Wasn't that Dinesh who had demanded to know, "What is she doing here with you?" when we drove up to the porch, and I was clinging to Rumi Bhai in tears and wouldn't let go even after we had stopped? Didn't Rumi Bhai say, "Get Bilquis now and then fetch the rations before the store closes" in a voice I had forgotten he had until today? And hadn't Dinesh said, "Be very careful," but had gone all the same? What is clearer is sitting in the galvanized iron tub with Bilquis and the daughter that I never knew she had, soaping and scrubbing me and sluicing buckets of water over my head.

"Oh Raheela beti, what did they do to you?"

The water had turned the colour of rust. I did not lose the smell even after two hours in the tub and with three changes of water. My face was tender and swollen. My eyes teared for three days. I couldn't eat. I vomited the hot milk that Rumi Bhai brought himself when I was in bed. My memories return.

Hanif Chacha is grabbing Munna's arm trying to stop him.

"Arrey, begum, let her go. It was nothing. Let it be. Ashfaq, for God's sake. Listen to me. Let her go. She is just a child."

"I should have pounded my belly until she aborted. How can I have given birth to such a whore? I curse the day she was born," Ammi says.

Papa is puffy and red. He is uttering obscenities coldly. Such filth. Ammi has wiped her fingers on my shalwar. She leans across and drubs me with her fists in a fit of crying that is nearer to laughter. Her bangles cut my forehead. I can feel something warm ooze down my cheekbone. Her hair is in my eyes and nose.

She spits in my face.

"Whore."

It was the blue room, but it did not register with me in my shock. The fan was flyblown and black. The steel almirah had been dented on one side as if someone had taken a hammer to the lock. I traced the dust on the cabinet, and heard what I thought was a mouse squeak and run in the canvas straps. What else do I remember?

I am screaming but I choke. Vomit trickles down the side of my mouth where the gag has shifted. My stomach is heaving despite the weight. I fear I have lost control of my bowels.

"What in God's name is going on? Have you all gone mad? Ashfaq, what is the meaning of this? Suresh, Selma, unhand her at once. Hanif Bhai, please ring Hashim Siddiqui at the police headquarters. Lahol bilaquwat, your own child."

The voice is feebler, but from the first click of the jaw I know that he is here. I faint.

I had stayed close to him. I remember I had gripped his arm when I tried to explain between fits of sobbing. I kept wiping my nose and face. When he had listened, he held me close.

"Let's get you a bath first and some food, and then we'll talk some more," Rumi Bhai said, looking at me with his kind eyes.

After the bath, I went out again to the verandah, a little calmer. He was in the chair, and Dinesh was standing over him with a paper in his hand. Dinesh left grudgingly when I appeared. Rumi Bhai answered, "Nothing, just some paperwork," when I asked him what was the matter, but his eyes were fearful. We sat in the twilight looking at the sunset over where the fields used to be. The garden was full of weeds, and the orchard the colour of straw. The rosery had been dug to make room for a large clay-and-wattle hut.

This is a lie. I have kept things from you. I didn't mean to, but there are many sketches that I have hidden. I didn't trust anyone enough, not even you. I still don't.

It had happened when he came to see his brother play in that match. We had agreed to meet in Company Bagh that evening. I had sneaked out, saying that I was going to see Suman. I met him in the grove.

"Did you know that Rumi Bhai donated these deodars from his garden? He used to tell us these stories about this place. Did you hear about this Englishman whose ghost still haunts the place? Apparently, he appears at midnight asking for 'whiskey-doubleroti.' Tommy..."

"Raheela, why can't we just run away?" Vivek asks.

"Where?" I say, feeling lost.

"Anywhere. I can get a job in Australia or Canada after I finish. So can you."

"I don't know. Why don't we wait and see?"

"You kept telling me that in Kanpur. What's to see?"

There is a cough and a rustle on the ground behind us. I am alert at once. My heart is beating fast and my chest feels constricted.

"Who was it? Did you see?"

"Not sure. One of the Hidayatullah boys. Khalid, I think."

"We'd better go."

Yes, there are other frames. Huddling in my strange outfit in the train, the relief when the train moves, the panic, falling into Vivek's arms at the station. The scandalized look on the driver's face. Nuzhat Nani and her kindness and her grandson Suhael. The civil wedding. Vivek troubleshooting as a computer consultant in the day and studying at night. My work at a travel agency and drawing lessons. I cannot bring myself to touch paints. After a month, we move to Yamuna Vihar and keep moving. The threatening calls at home and to my places of work, and birthday cards from Rumi Bhai with always a thousand-rupee note and some news. Papa needs a bypass. The hut in Sassurkhaderi was set on fire. No one knows. No deaths or injuries. Selma, pregnant again. Suraiya, her youngest, has a heart problem. Flying to London for the operation.

Ms. Ashfaq's set piece or colophon is a diptych of a hawk's moth, its downy wings pinned to sandalwood. Inset are skeins of silk thread from a wig and a shellacked, pressed rose. In the second panel, a transparency of van Gogh's death's head oil is imposed on a charcoal sketch of the artist's family as if attending at the base of the crucifixion...

We are now in Bangalore. I am expecting. It's a girl. I call her Mona. I try to understand this grave, silent creature that I have given birth to. Flesh of my flesh. A child who never cries at night like other infants. Sometimes, I come across her scrawls with their images of war and death when other children her age spend their hours playing with dolls. Mona stays quiet for days. When she is three, Vivek is accepted at Macquarie University.

The postscripts are short and difficult. There are various counsellors and psychiatrists, wards and crisis rooms, many hospitals. Can I forget the doctor screaming, "serves you right," as I choke on the tube the nurse uses to empty my stomach? ("Don't pay attention to her, dear. She's mean to everyone," says the nurse.) I cut my body with safety razors but I don't remember doing it. It's always hardest when Vivek is away. My poor Mona. I relax by mapping the cadence of images and objects. What they call my art.

The day of the departure. A surprise. He is riding pillion on his nephew Suhael's scooter, clinging to him. God, he's grown so weak. I am shocked he managed to make it here. His eyes seem cloudy and his step falters. What is it? We don't talk much. I don't ask about home. He promises to turn things the way they were. I know they can't be. He strokes my forehead and then charms Mona into animation. My first tears in years. This is my final sketch in the series. Not in sequence. He is on the scooter. It circles our car like a seagull on our way to the airport. He has on a white cloth hat. A raised hand after we are past the ticket counter. A last wave. No goodbyes. We are through.

Dearest Apa, Selma writes, *I hope this finds you as well as we are here. All the children want to know when you will come again. I think all of them are "gone" on Vivek. We took Suraiya to the heart institute last month. The cardiologist thinks that she is stable and out of danger but that we should monitor against infections and the like. Her immune system is still suppressed, and she catches things easily. We'll have to move to the hills soon, although I have to be very careful in case my bronchitis flares up and causes complications for her. We are keeping our fingers crossed and doing our best. The rest is not up to us, of course, but we are fervently praying that everything will be all right. Mehbooba Khala is well, although her sciatica flares up in cooler weather.*

Apa, Ammi, and Papa are well too, given their ages. They send you their love. It is difficult, though, to get Papa to follow any doctor's advice. He always seems to know better. You know how he is. The last of the immortals, or so he thinks. He spends a lot of time in the back room, reading and playing chess with Suresh, who sometimes comes with his wife, Anusha, Mrs. Sarkar's middle daughter.

Six months ago, Mrs. Hidayatullah's father died in his farmhouse in Mehrauli. Auntie told Ammi that when she went for the funeral she uncovered ligature marks on his neck as if he had been strangled. The neighbours and some developers tried to lay claim to the property. Somehow, Auntie managed to get the house and the valuables after she got Siddiqui Sahib and Mr. Maudwell, Billa Sahib, to go there. Billa Sahib sent some strongmen later. Khalid is now living there and taking care of it. There is a police constable on the premises.

We hadn't seen Rumi Bhai in ages and neither had any of his other friends. These days, he doesn't come very often. When he did surface eventually last month, he admitted, rather shamefacedly, that he had been hiding in his basement for a week as soon as he heard that a space station was due to fall on earth within days. The dear man looked ill, weak, and harried…

⁂

Vivek tells me that I am cynical and that it's time, not rupiyahs or dollars, that has done the trick. The threats and phone calls had stopped once we moved from country to country for research or teaching and he was appointed a full professor and I had my first exhibition in Yokohama and sold my assemblages and sketches and started sending money home. Since then, I've held shows in Shanghai, Dresden, Versailles, Bombay, Tokyo, São Paolo, Lagos, Bangalore, and Český Krumlov. I just couldn't bring myself to sketch anything on my last trips home. Those cold, calculated welcomes. I could not bear to be touched, except by the children. The visits home have been awful, but I have not cried.

⁂

It's always after the lights are out and the room hums with night that panic floods my mind, tossing thoughts aside and back like flotsam from a wreck. The night uncovers some strange forms in the depths of my mind, scuttling like crabs or wriggling like sea snakes under sand.

No paints here. The smell makes me feel as if I am peering down a gorge. The canvas is stretched too tightly on the easel. It will rip from the stress. I know. Nothing can be done now.

Sleep is gone. My world is without definition. I am walking through a fog, bumping into shapes. Outstretched hands grope, blunder, and guess their way into sense. But how can I grasp or change the past? It's a murky country. It confuses me. It keeps fusing with the present. I keep my sketchbooks propped against the wall to help me remember, but did I ever paint these images that I recall now the way they were? The woman in the bed to my left cries at night for her daughter who doesn't visit. Mona is coming. I can hear her clip-clop in the hall and Vivek's voice answering Pammi.

When do I wake up?

BOOK REVIEW

On the Edge of My Seat: Test Highlights from Around the World
By Henry Blofeld. 177 pp. London et alia: Stanley Paul & Co., 1991.
$24.95 09-1748720

To:
Dr. J.M. Brearley
Marylebone Cricket Club
St. John's Wood
London NW8

Dear Dr. Brearley,

Fräulein Harron forwarded for analysis a brown paper parcel that contained a singular case history of hysteria. I have consulted with my colleagues in Wien and Leipzig, and we feel this case is best handled by you. I understand you are a practising psychotherapist and deal with cricketitis in all its aberrations. I believe you were also captain of the English cricket team, but we will not hold that against you. Please treat the matter with professional confidence. The facts are as follows:

Abandoned one day by his father who disappears into the "long" room at Lord's, child Blofeld—obviously an alias, the name sounds too much like one of Ian Fleming's villains to be true—spends the rest of his life looking for thrills on the cricket field. He develops alarming symptoms as a result of this childhood episode. He confesses to arousal at the sight of the "exciting bagginess of the dark green Australian caps," and the thought of Cowdrey (whose batting he found "deep, dark, and mysterious") at the non-striker's end still leaves him "limp with excitement" twenty-eight years on.

But all is not flaccidity for young detumescent "Blowers" or "Blowfly," as he is also called. He favours Dexter who is "upright and handsome," and Hutton's deeds move him to discharge his duty. (For "Hutton" read "mutton" to clarify the subject's link to carnality and satyriasis.) Waiting in the dressing room at Lord's for the Eton vs. Harrow game, and "sitting on those leather sofas and thinking of the illustrious bums that had sat there down the years," the subject Blofeld is stimulated by smells that have an uplifting effect on him. He decides to call the description of his symptoms "On the Edge of My Seat." (More on this posterior fetish later.)

Not surprisingly, the subject Blofeld exhibits various amphigenic inversion traits. He is clearly repelled by a spectatrix's offer of marriage on the Hill at Sydney. (The location is self-evidently significant.) As we suspected, he admits that his favourite ground lies in the heart of "Middlesex" for some barely concealed reason but, in mitigation, admits being highly excited on other grounds in other countries. At Trent Bridge, Blofeld dreams of the "lovely, hirsute characters" who formed the Nottingham professional corps in the last century. The picture of a nude seaman jumping over the stumps at Lord's is included in the book—it is heavily smudged—and although I have not glanced at this more than five times to check the facts, I feel this piece of evidence confirms my final analysis.

The subject Blofeld stays shy of the female sex, although he recounts the touching story of Kim Hughes in tears after she is relieved of the Australian captaincy. Bev Congdon is also remembered for her fighting qualities. He cannot disguise his admiration for the Amazonian feats of that femme fatale Viv Richards. The subject Blofeld is occupied with the BBC—which he denies stands for "big-breasted chatelaines"—he claims that it is a radio station, but then persists in calling it "auntie." Surely, a diagnosis of arrested submissiveness is the only explanation here, if we may be allowed to be accurate, but imprecise. (In fairness to Blofeld, we have heard him speak, and this part of his story may be true, as his pronunciation is not as bad as it sounds.)

The subject writes beautifully in a crabbed, Teutonic style that led us to compare him favourably with our own Hölderlin. How sublime the "one imagined technicians frantically twiddling knobs in Australia as well as England. Then the miracle occurred, the static died down, and, wonderful to relate, the Australian voice of, say, Alan McGilvray would come floating into the dark, cold bedroom" is, yes? However, in the throes of twiddling knobs with febrile excitement, the divine Blofeld mistakes "Randell" for "Randall" (p.94); on p.105 "Ewen" becomes "Euan"; and "huge," "hugh" on p.137. Blofeld becomes so distraught at the sight of a huge West Indian (not hugh) with plump hocks carrying off his beloved Cowdrey from the field that he misspells "Jamaica" on p.152. Much is made of the way the "Pegasus Hotel" is pronounced in the Caribbean.

I am aware of Sir Adrian Stokes's monumental contribution to the psychoanalysis of ball games, in which he described cricketers as a fraternity held in an agonistic engagement like the nude wrestlers of Greece. Sir Adrian's insight is deep when he claims that the batsman who is caught out suffers symbolic castration, but nothing in his oeuvre prepares us for such deviations as the subject Blofeld narrates. The recital of such unregenerate filth makes Barbusse, de Sade, and Restif de la Bretonne sound like temperance sermons for backward infants in perambulators. (I do not know about taping his commentaries. They should certainly think about taping his mouth.) Faced with cases like these, I have often considered resigning from the profession altogether. Your kind assistance and expertise will keep me going.

Please convey my regards to Herr Doktor, Mama Freud, and little Anna. I recall well our last meal together. Roast beef and Yorkshire pudding with custard—or was it mustard? I cannot remember. Jung sends his salaams. Adler injured one of his chins and is accusing Krafft–Ebing of unconscious hostility. These babies.

I am
Yours, etc.
Mechmedt von Samiullahus

P.S. You will excuse my writing to you in English, but it is good practice for me to keep the tongue on its toes.

(Mechmedt von Samiullahus is the owner of Kitabgarh and the editor of *The Oklahoman Cricketer*.)

THE GUEST

Huma had gone mad. Or so Mrs. Siddiqui feared. At dawn, while the household was still asleep, her daughter would get up and pray without stopping for four hours. When it was time to study, she would open her textbook on hygrophilous micro-organisms and weep aloud with her head in her hands. When someone tried to speak to her, she would gaze away or smile without answering.

Lately, her behaviour had become even odder. When they sat down to lunch, she would start humming the bagpipe tunes that the St. Marry's Parade Band played at the police lines every Sunday. Worse, sometimes, she brought a comb with oiled paper to the table and used that to pipe her tunes through. Mr. Siddiqui's attempts to take it away from her usually ended in hysterics.

When she was feeling particularly happy, Huma would venture into "Loch Maree" and "Mrs. John MacColl" but, usually, it was a skirling medley of "Lochaber No More," "Leaving Barra," "Deil in the Kitchen," and "The Taking of

Beaumont Hamel" that they got. At the end, Huma would cling to the houseboys and sob until they pried her loose and locked her in her room.

Her mother was at her wit's end. After a particularly heart-rending performance of "God Save the King," which Huma had performed standing up over the roghan josh, Mrs. Siddiqui said to her husband:

"Listen, Hashim, I don't know how you feel. I could put up with the praying and the crying, but this music will drive me mad. After all those music lessons we gave her, can't she at least pick someone else like Sehgal or Munni Begum, or play a nice ghazal or a raag once in a while, instead of all this heehawing through the nose? And hugging that fat Madrasi cook, that was too much. It's high time that madam was married off. That's what I think."

She continued, "Whoever heard of an unmarried twenty-eight-year-old? People will think there's something wrong with her."

Spiritedly, Mr. Siddiqui countered that it was just Huma's nerves brought on by overwork.

"Let's not be hasty. Why don't we wait till her *viva* is over? She'll be fine. It's all those labs, the experiments, you know, the microtomy. It can get stressful. You know, she was always sensitive. Remember the time she saw me squash that caterpillar in the kitchen sink? She was so upset for a week that she wouldn't eat even when I tried to feed her."

"You've always spoiled her, Hashim," Mrs. Siddiqui said to her husband. "She's almost thirty. Old. Not a baby anymore. It's your fault she never got married. Who wants a girl with a doctorate in semi-argillaceous and psammous-soil microphytes, whatever they are? All that studying. Scares people off. You take this lenient attitude with everyone. No wonder the criminals are running riot in this city."

Mr. Siddiqui's police training told him that he was outgunned and surrounded. He retreated to the tune of the reveille that Huma was now sounding through the comb.

During this exchange, Mr. Siddiqui's mother had shuffled in. She opened her paan box on the takhat and passed her hand over her upper lip, stroking the growth lovingly. He noticed that her stoop was getting worse.

"Nonsense, Hashim. It's not study or nerves if you ask me," his mother concluded.

"Ammajan, what is it?"

"Simple. The girl's possessed."

"Possessed, really, Ammajan," Mr. Siddiqui protested. "It's just a phase. It'll pass."

"It happened to Bablu Chacha too. That was before your time. A djinni had taken over him. He was a wicked one. Hashim bete, remember what I told you when she was born. She had that mark on her forehead exactly where that old rascal, your Bablu Chacha, did. It's his sins that she's carrying."

"Ammajan, that's just a naevus. We had that checked. It's common in a family. Sometimes skips a generation or two. There's nothing unusual about it. I'll take her to the doctor first. She probably needs some B12 injections. Too much reading and computers."

"You mark my words, you with your mavis, naevus. Give her all the B12s and B52s you want. I've lived a lot longer than you have and have seen things you won't believe, Mr. Policeman. If you ask me, I think it's that Ashfaq woman. She always was the spiteful type. She was so envious when Huma topped the school while her daughters were playing the fool. Her cook told the driver that she sits in the evening on the takhat in her green room with her head covered, and rocks back and forth and curses everyone for hours, the witch."

"Ammajan, really, you shouldn't listen to servants' gossip. That's all nonsense. It's time to get past all this."

"No lime. They took that too. Last time it was my betel nuts. Thieves. You're right, dear, Hashim can't catch them but I will," Ammajan said.

Under her breath, Mrs. Siddiqui asked her husband, "Look, can't you ask Ammajan to shave once in a while?"

"What, how do you expect me to do that? Why me? Can't you do it?" Mr. Siddiqui protested.

"She's your mother. I'll start asking around. I'll start with Razia's marriage bureau first, and see what she says. I'll take Ammajan to look for some nice fabric for shalwar kameezes for Huma, none of this pinafore and jeans business. Buy some Fair and Lovely to clear her complexion too. The marriage market is tough. Hard for a twenty-eight-year-old girl. Anyway, Hashim, you take Huma to that doctor."

Mr. Siddiqui wheeled the motorcycle out of the garage. Huma walked behind and, when the machine started, hopped on and rode pillion. They went past the Willingdon Club and the university in the old town towards the cantonment. As they weaved through chowk, Huma drew wolf whistles from the paanshop loafers. Oh, for God's sake, no. Huma was giggling and waving to these louts. She even hummed a few bars of "Highland Laddie." Maybe the good lady was right. It was high time Huma was married off.

They pulled up in front of a yellow concrete wall with a barred gate. The sign read, "Dr. Gupta's Medical and Psycho Centre." A chowkidaar, a powerfully built man now run to seed, stiffened to attention with his lathi at his side. He opened the gate. The motorcycle tore down the driveway of red gravel and drew up in the portico.

"Doctor sahib in?" boomed Mr. Siddiqui to the chowkidaar who had followed.

"Yes, sir, yes, sir, come in, doctor back in five minutes. Lady coming." He had big ears and a slash for a mouth. "Arrey, Govind."

The old servant ushered them into the waiting area. The chairs in the waiting area were big and uncomfortable. There was a smell of sandalwood from the incense burner. Two rows of flying wooden ducks on the wall converged in a > that soared towards the transom.

A door opened and a woman in a sari and a tilak entered. They did their namastes. Huma was quiet as her father explained.

"It is good that you have come. My husband believes that it is important to include the family in the therapy. Maybe your good wife should also come. Yes, I agree, there is such a shortage of this kind of help in this city, in India also." To Huma, she said, "Haan, beti, what will you drink? Coca-Cola, tea, Pee Cola, Fanta?"

Huma said yes to everything. Mrs. Gupta went inside. They heard her order tea, Coca-Cola, and namkeens.

While they were talking, the doctor walked in twenty-five minutes later. The chowkidaar followed with the golf bag.

"Siddiqui Sahib, sorry, the Chief Surgeon wanted an extra hole or two. He was losing, you see. Ah, this is the young lady. Huma, what a pretty name. How are you?"

Huma giggled and said, "Gowf."

"Did you like the Coca-Cola? Another one for Miss Huma?"

She nodded, giggling shyly.

"Let's go into the office, Miss Huma, and you too, Siddiqui Sahib."

The doctor began by asking her medical history. Huma spoke of her ovarian cysts and other ailments. The doctor was impressed. He made notes and looked at her once or twice, saying, "How interesting." Mr. Siddiqui was relieved that she was lucid.

Next, he felt her pulse, auscultated the heart, took her blood pressure, and tapped her knees. Her legs shot out with amazing speed and caught him on both shins.

"Nothing wrong with her reflexes," he said, rubbing his shins, "but heart's racing a bit. Any broken bones in the past?" A shake of the head.

"Good. How about breathing problems? Tight jaw?"

"Yes, she grinds her teeth but she's stopped talking to us really. Very distressing," Mr. Siddiqui responded.

"She's probably just run down. BP's high. Stress, probably. I'll give her something for that. I'd like to run some tests on her. Not physical."

Dr. Gupta showed Huma some ink blots on paper and asked for her reactions. She was slow to respond, shaking her head, but then started shouting "butterflies" and made some other guttural noises. The doctor peered over his glasses at her while scribbling on the pad and nodded to Mr. Siddiqui.

"Not important what she's saying, but she is talking. That's a good sign," Dr. Gupta said.

Huma looked slyly at both in turn, her eyes shining.

Next he said, "I will say a word and you respond with another. Is that clear?"

"Word association. That I know," said Mr. Siddiqui triumphantly.

Huma looked bored.

"Child"

"Bastard"

A reproving "Huma!" from Mr. Siddiqui earned him a lecture from the doctor.

"You know, this Psycho Centre operates on some principles. That means accepting that some things that the patient will say will shock you. I tell this to everyone. I must ask you, Siddiqui Sahib, to be as quiet as possible."

"Sorry, Doctor. It's just that nobody in the family uses language like that. Don't know where she could have picked it up."

"Okay, Huma?" Dr. Gupta began.

She nodded.

"Apple"

"Pommage"

"Money"

"Skive"
"Hen"
"Gallus"
"Dog"
"Glaikit"
"Whale"
"Maukit"
"Ah." He wrote something down.
"Is that significant?" Mr. Siddiqui asked.
"May be," said Dr. Gupta and continued:
"Egypt"
"Steamin'"
"Flower"
"Braw"
"Mother"
"Besom"
"Father"
"Fouter"
"Sister"

Huma cried but signalled a little later to say that she was ready to continue.

"Summer"
"Wabbit"
"Children"
"Scunners"

"I've never heard those before," admitted Mr. Siddiqui. "What do they mean? Are they medical terms?"

The doctor shook his head.

The exchange had animated Huma. She talked normally with the doctor until it was time to go. As soon as the doctor observed that she hadn't hummed, she promptly launched into "Paddy's Leather Breeches." Her eyes glittered unhealthily.

"Doctor, we don't know what to do, my wife and I," Mr. Siddiqui admitted.

The doctor gave his diagnosis.

"It is clear that she has some nervous strain. She needs rest. Of course, there is deep-seated hostility towards parental authority figures. Her ego is in a state of dejection, and there is some confusion about her sexuality. Her self-esteem needs to be built up. But first, we must get her physically well. The rest will follow," Dr. Gupta concluded.

He wrote out a prescription for a course of vitamin injections and Waterbury's Compound, and explained some of his theories.

Huma said her goodbyes to the Guptas, who came to see them out. The doctor called out.

"Chowkidaar, show sahib and memsahib the way to the dispensary. Goodbye, Miss Huma."

Huma suddenly turned, with an arm on her hip, and said in a vampy tone to the chowkidaar, "Arrey, where have you been? I have been looking for you all my life. I want to marry you. Let's do that soon. Bye bye, darling. Phir milenge."

Scandalized, Mr. Siddiqui threw a deprecating grin at the doctor and quickened his step, dragging Huma along. The chowkidaar twirled his moustache and turned his head occasionally to watch Huma dreamily as he walked ahead.

However, when they reached the dispensary and Huma saw the compounder take out the hypodermic syringe, she fled into the street in tears with her father racing after her. When they returned, she trembled and shook in her father's arms, her face averted, as the plunger went in. She seemed to become calm and sleepy after that. She seemed to have forgotten altogether about the chowkidaar. They went home.

Husband and wife conversed.

"I think you're right, dear. Can't we find a good boy for her quickly?" Mr. Siddiqui asked.

"Why, what did the doctor say?" Mrs. Siddiqui prodded.

"I didn't understand most of it. Something about authority and dejection and sexual confusion. Apparently, parents create these problems by getting their children to compete with each other at school. Suddenly, one child is held up to be better than the others. This creates a sense of inferiority and a lack of contact with the real person, which leads to the mental equilibrium shifting. That's what he said, I think," Mr. Siddiqui concluded.

"Arrey, didn't you tell him that she's an only child?" Mrs. Siddiqui asked.

"I tried but he seemed to go on and on about dysfunctional families. I think he even mentioned the India–Pakistan conflict in those terms."

"Bloody fool. Crazies at that Psycho Centre. I just felt it in my bones. Don't go there again."

"Yes, dear, I won't be going anywhere, except to Kheri in the hunting season to see Dhillon. Some problems."

Mrs. Siddiqui's visit to the marriage bureau had gone better than expected. Razia, the bureau owner, had asked for all the details and had promised the description would be circulated soon ("such an intelligent girl, the mark is very faint, not a problem"). She drafted a notice:

> Muslim girl, 28, DPhil candidate,
> tall, attractive, intelligent, musical,
> good family, wishes to meet boy 30–40,
> English-educated, secure professional.
> Matrimony only. No dowry.
>
> Send cv to:
>
> Heart-to-Heart Matrimonials
> 143/4–Cariappa Circle
> Mumfordganj, UP

Razia returned three weeks later with some cvs. Some were from young bucks who described themselves as deep-chested and boasted of their singing voice. There was a doctor from Rourkela and a dentist with a stammer. Another manufactured Rubik's cubes in Bangalore. One candidate had turned down twelve job offers at various American and European universities to teach at home.

Some suitors came in person. Huma was well-behaved throughout. However, at the seventh sitting, she broke into the opening bars of "Barren Rocks of Aden." The boy seemed amused, but his family looked bewildered and left hastily. When Mrs. Siddiqui called the bureau, Razia was matter-of-fact. She advised her to take Huma out of town for a long rest at once. This way, people might forget; otherwise, people would talk. Mrs. Siddiqui felt frustrated. In the meantime, word must have spread because the offers dried up as Razia had predicted.

Meanwhile, the course of injections had not produced any improvements. It was clear that Huma would not be able to complete her studies. Her antics continued.

Nevertheless, Mrs. Siddiqui persevered. She set out the next day in the car with Ammajan and Huma for the shoe shop. At the store, the thin and nervous shoe seller looked agape as Ammajan doffed her burkha.

"Ammajan," hissed Mrs. Siddiqui in a whisper, "when was the last time you shaved?"

"I used to do it daily when Salim was alive. Since he died, I have nobody left to shave for. Why do you ask?" said her mother-in-law.

Huma pulled the shawl over her head shyly like a bride, made sheep's eyes at the salesman, and stuck out her tongue at him.

"Ram, Ram," said the man, jumping away to shelve the shoe.

Mrs. Siddiqui made a quick decision. Shouting "Ammajan, come," she pulled Huma to her feet and raced to find the car. Her social certitudes were deserting her. She felt like screaming.

"This is it," she confided later to her friend Mrs. Pandey. "I think I'll go mad before she does."

"Don't say such things, yaar. Not even as a joke. Arrey, this new baba, have you heard of him? Pulls vibhuti out of the air, cures all kinds. Jadoo mantar. Miracles. Religion, no bar. Treats everyone, yaar, Muslims, Sikhs, what have you, even Christians. I'm taking Suman there. Wish something for Suman, na. Fat, fat she has become. Going to the fridge every hour only. What can I do? Marriage next year. Why not Huma, haan?"

Mrs. Siddiqui thought about it and nodded, and said she would do it. "Better than all these Psycho Centre nutters."

Mrs. Siddiqui took the police jeep to the riverbank. The road was packed with pilgrims. She pursed her lips when she saw hippies swaying to some music.

"Chee, chee, look at their hair."

"Ji, begum sahib, they are taking charas," suggested the driver.

"And that girl is almost naked. Prinking in her brassiere. So dirty. Mlecch. Lahol bilaquwat. Chalo, driver, get us there quickly."

The driver honked ferociously, and the sea of the faithful and the curious parted before the chariot.

"God, how many people are here? So much religion, but why so much thievery then in this city? What can poor Hashim do by himself, I ask you?"

They parked in front of the fort where pilgrims told their beads, waited for alms, or went for a dip in the river.

"There are millions of people here. Driver, where is he?"

"Inside the temple, begumsahib."

"Kahaan hain swamiji?"

A volunteer with a large bag and ribbons on his chest pointed at the fort.

"Chalo, Huma," said Mrs. Siddiqui.

They passed a group of sadhus with topknots, clad in nothing but ash from head to foot, their grey penises swinging with each stride. Huma turned and waved. One smiled and wiggled his trishul. Mrs. Siddiqui pulled Huma violently after her without saying a word.

They passed the banyan tree, whose roots twined round the sculptures of gods and goddesses, and went downstairs. The gallery was filled with incense and the sounds of chanting and the clang of metal on metal. They filed past the Hanuman devotees to the crowd in front of the basalt naag where the baba sat dressed simply on a yellow cotton sheet. He looked bald and frail, and the sacred thread across his distended belly fluttered as he swayed from time to time.

"Near samadhi. The baba has fasted for thirty days now," someone whispered.

Mrs. Siddiqui watched him rub some ash on a thin boy whose face twitched convulsively. After reciting some slokas, he signalled for the boy to be removed. The boy's mother stepped forward, her eyes shining with hope. She gratefully folded her hands and tried to touch his feet, but the attendant pointed to the bowl. She fumbled at a knot in the sari, and dropped a stream of bills and coins into his bowl, which the helper scooped away.

After a wait, it was their turn. The baba was plainly weary.

"Haan beti, do not worry. You will be well soon."

He closed his eyes in prayer. He put one hand on Huma's forehead as he told the beads with the other. Huma was calm. He whispered something to the attendant, who took her aside and gave her two packets.

"Take this vibhuti and this kheer," the attendant said to Mrs. Siddiqui. "Smear it all over the child who must lie naked on poornima under a full moon till dawn. She must think pure thoughts. Get her to eat the kheer. Three hundred rupees."

She gave the money.

"And some for the baba. More, for the temple. Can't you give any more?"

When that night came, a screen was erected around the cot. The curious children who gathered were dispersed by a few slaps and shouts from the constables. Huma gagged on the taste of ashes in the kheer. She undressed, and Mrs. Siddiqui applied the vibhuti. Huma lay on the hard bed that cold night, wondering if there were plants on the moon.

In the morning, they rushed her to the Bayley Hospital. Dr. Jeejeebhoy was furious as he put away the stethoscope.

"You should know better, Mrs. Siddiqui. Sadhus, really. No medicinal value. Pneumonia. Full-blown. Look at the blennorrhoea. Give her these antibiotics. No more lying naked under the full moon in winter, either with pure or impure thoughts. No more quackery, please. She's your daughter, after all. What are you people thinking?"

Meenakshi, Huma's friend, had another idea.

"Auntie," she said, "Rohinton and Nilufer's mother has the magic chapatti. So many people have been cured. I think we should take Huma. No, no, it won't do any harm. Absolutely not. Who knows, it might actually help."

Reluctantly, Mrs. Siddiqui agreed.

At the house, the chapatti was brought out in a metal dish covered with a lace doily. Nilufer's mother told Mrs. Siddiqui that she had to sip two tablespoons of the water in which the roti floated to be followed by six Hail Marys at night. The cure would take eight weeks. Huma was cooperative and went to her friend's place every week, but there wasn't any improvement.

"Probably some other influence at work," hinted Nilufer's mother. "Dear Huma, save her from evil. Such an intelligent girl. So sweet. God bless."

Ammajan finally decided to call the maulvi. He arrived in the evening, a man of about forty, slender with a goatish countenance, dressed in a chikkun kurta and pajamas. He had one grey eye, the other black. His beard was stained with attar. He kept his head down and listened to them with what Mrs. Siddiqui described as false modesty. She suspected him of vanity. She did not like the man although she agreed to his proposal. She couldn't see why she had to pay the odious man his five hundred rupees before the work had even started.

When the day arrived, the household was prepared. The servant fetched the ropes from the shed. The maulvi ordered Mr. Siddiqui and Mrs. Siddiqui to bind Huma to the chair in the storeroom. Huma screamed and fought back when they cornered her. Ammajan brought some glowing-coal incense from the kitchen on a silver platter. The maulvi sahib only permitted Ammajan to stay.

Outside the door, they heard the muttered suras. The scent of the lobaan wafted into the corridor through the door slats, but they did not dare peek in. The recitation went on for half an hour. Then the beatings and screaming started, and a conversation began in weird voices.

"It was scary," Ammajan told her son later. "When he stopped reading from the Koran, Huma started growling strangely in this deep voice. I said, 'Wait, Mr. Broome's aunt talks like that. Let me get Huma's mother. She'll know.'"

Mrs. Siddiqui entered the room. The maulvi sahib resumed the beatings with the sandals as Huma writhed and cried.

Then, a fine baritone issued from Huma's lips, telling the maulvi to stop hurting her.

"Who are you?" the maulvi asked.

"Dinnae get yersel' in a fankle, Macgregor. Ye sound like a right crabbit blether."

"What is he saying?" asked the maulvi.

"Truly, this is the devil's language," said Ammajan, awed.

"Oh Iblees, get thee gone," said the maulvi, brandishing the holy book like a flail.

Mrs. Siddiqui raised her hand to silence them and asked, "Who are you?"

"It's only Callum McCallum here, mum, born o' the Clyde, but down from the hi'lands at yer service, yer grace." He did a few bars of "Cock o' the North."

"Where are you from and what do you want, Callum McCallum?" she asked.

"Called me a treuchter, these clydesiders, 'cause when I was a tiddler I shucked a few trout older than his mum, no disrespect meant. Grand food is parritch, grand food."

"And just why are you tormenting my daughter? Have you no manners?"

"Tormenting? I? Oh, my love, she's but a lassie yet, my love, she's but a lassie yet. For there the bonie lassie lives, the lassie I lo'e best. Let me sing something."

Mrs. Siddiqui took a direct approach to her daughter's guest who had finished "Piper of Drummond" and "High Road to Linton" and was halfway through "Teribus." She drew a deep breath and let it out with a force that shook the curtains, Ammajan said later to her son.

"Shut your gob," Mrs. Siddiqui snapped.

The singing quailed to a stop.

"Let me do this," said the maulvi quietly.

When the maulvi asked him to leave Huma, the voice replied cuttingly.

"Don't be meir daft, man. Why should I? I like the wee woman. Ye cannae shift a chindit sae easily."

The beatings started again, and that voice said something: "Spairges about the brunstane cootie, to scaud poor wretches."

The guest began singing again.

"'O, lay thy loof in mine, lass, in mine, lass, in mine, lass.'"

Mrs. Siddiqui decided that enough was enough. She grabbed the sandal and started to drub Huma.

(rit.) "I'm her mother. Go back to your stinking Glasgow," she said, timing each word with a blow.

She continued *(ff)*: "Leave my daughter alone," increasing the ferocity of the beatings.

There was a pause before the guest spoke again.

(p) "Oh, but can I at least visit her from time to time? Please?"

(mf) "No, go now."

(Plaintive, pp) "Oh, come on, ye cannae be so hard-hearted. I did say 'please.'"

(cresc.) "No, leave now. Or I'll come back to haunt you."

After a few well-aimed hits, it was (pp, dim.): "Oh, och, leave off, 'nuff, 'nuff, I go, I go."

Ammajan was shaking when she emerged with a tired, tousled Huma who was on the verge of collapse. The maulvi followed, running his fingers through his beard while he held the Koran in the right. He uttered a few duas before leaving, and blew over Huma several times. Mrs. Siddiqui was exhausted. Her husband took her to the living room where she sat on a maundha and drank tea. After applying some poultices to Huma, the ordeal was over, she figured.

It did not happen that way. Although Huma stopped her humming, she worsened. She tore at her hair and clothes in public. She frequently broke into fits of crying, and was rarely allowed out of the room. Every fortnight they took her to the Psycho Centre where Dr. Gupta administered electric shocks. These used to terrify her at first, but later she would limit herself to whimpering and huddling in the corner. Finally, Dr. Gupta said he could not do any more. He recommended that they commit her to the asylum in Agra.

He wrote to the asylum, and eighteen days later the director came in person to meet Huma at home. He seemed a kindly man, and Huma was quiet in his presence. He talked with Mrs. Siddiqui, who had packed Huma's suitcase. Huma got into the jeep with her father and the director without any trouble, and waved to her mother who blew her duas as they drove away.

Things get a little muddy at this stage. After Huma was sent away, Hashim Siddiqui was touring Kheri after the riots when his jeep was ambushed in the forest by dacoits. He was killed outright. Ammajan died two years later. Mrs. Siddiqui suffered a stroke some time after that, which left her right side paralyzed. Meanwhile, reports of Huma's progress continued to arrive from the asylum from time to time. She had improved over the last four years, the last seven, even the last twelve.

Finally, a letter arrived saying that she was fully stable and ought to be discharged from the asylum. Another came a month later. Both went unanswered. Finally, the director decided to bring Huma home himself. When he arrived, he explained to Mrs. Siddiqui that Huma could live a normal life at home. She could even resume her studies if she wished.

Huma looked nervous. At the director's urging, she walked with open arms to hug her mother but saw her flinch. Huma started crying, ran back, and clung to the director. Mrs. Siddiqui said it was obvious that she was still not well and that she certainly couldn't take care of her, but the director was firm in his view that she was stable and could live a normal family life with minimal care as long as she took her medication. He promised to visit her when he could.

There are many stories of what happened next. Everyone agrees that Huma became much worse. After a while, she rarely spoke and did not recognize anyone, including her friends who visited her. Eventually, she was kept chained to the bars of the bedroom window. The director, who was now an old man and had long since retired from the asylum, came to see her once. She did not recognize him, and the poor man went away saddened.

Huma lived for another three years and died a year after her mother succumbed to pleurisy-related complications.

THE SADNESS OF SNAKES

I remember him well.

Apa and I went with Hla Khine Kyi to the city to buy some parts for the transistor. As he came out of the shop, he put the radio to his misshapen ear and listened. He allowed us to listen too. We took turns. I liked the music, but then there were speeches. I was puzzled. Were there little men and women inside? I asked him.

"Little men and women? No, no. No, no."

He laughed and laughed.

Seeing that I was upset, he told us this story about how his ear was torn by this famous wrestler whom he had defeated. He had kicked and screamed and bitten. Back in the old days, he used to break ships when they became old and useless, but he had to leave the yard after he became allergic to water. Whenever a drop touched him, he changed colour, he said. Sometimes, he would go purple, sometimes blue. Only the mashaw-tsi flower could cure him. He had one stuck behind his ear. He took us to see the jumping cats in the market and laughed again and again.

Hla Khine Kyi also told us how he was swept up once by the yellow wind and carried for miles like a bird in a storm to another town. Shaking the dust off his clothes, he had walked right back to his village fifty miles away. Both his brothers had been carried off too. He had been to the moon. Half of it was dark where the little people lived and came out to play at night. He was hungry and cold there, so he had decided to fly back.

Then he showed us his tattoo of a mermaid whose breasts grew bigger and jiggled when he flexed his muscles. He laughed and then solemnly rolled down his shirtsleeve. She was gone. He squatted. He took a cheroot from behind his other ear, lit it, and watched the street. His narrowed gaze lingered on the washerwomen carrying their loads.

"Hey," he called out, "looks like you need a good man." They waved their battledores threateningly. He laughed and smoked some more.

Earlier, he had taken us to the mill. He left on some errand while Daddy gave us samosas and tea and rasgullas in his office. Later, we watched the sugar canes being unloaded and mashed. There were stacks of husks in the warehouses. The place was full of buzzing flies. We watched the vats and the drying process, and held our noses against the stink of sulphur.

The day before, we had eaten a lot, tearing strips off the canes, or getting the servants to strip and dice them as we sat on the newspapers on the floor and chewed away, swallowing the syrup and licking our fingers. At times, someone would press out the sweet essence, add lemon juice and some rock salt, and give it to us in a glass. It was so refreshing. But how it stank when they refined it into white sugar in the mill. Why couldn't they leave it alone? In the alley next to the exit, there was that strong rotting smell of sugar. It clung to our clothes and our hair. And there were more flies and dogs lapping in the gutters. I didn't like going there.

We had gone to the Ramlila after the crushing. We had reached the open square. Near the flagpole, there were some Indians, a few dignitaries, and, next to a British officer, a hard-jawed man in an achkan, with spectacles screwed on tight. He spoke in a rumbling accent as he hoisted a tricoloured flag. Beside him stood a woman, fair and fat, in a green silk sari, her plaits braided with jasmine. His wife, perhaps. There were four girls behind her, large-nosed, long-haired with brown eyes.

"Oh, look at their blouses. Beautiful lace, and that colour. Must be expensive," I said.

"Khwe kala," Hla Khine Kyi snorted, more to himself, "we'll get rid of these black dogs. The day will come soon."

A moon hung over the night like a lantern. I remember the procession of that pink and green Ravana, lit and dying in flames and perishing in a hissing sea. It was the week before Daddy sent us away to the village.

·

We had just returned from paddling in the pool. Apa and I were splashing each other, trying not to get our blouses wet. Thambi, a little Tamil orphan of five whom Mummy had picked up along the way, began bawling when his bamboo boat was swept away in the stream. Apa waded in the water, hoisting her lungi, but it was gone. I gave Thambi a sesame ball to keep him quiet. He ate it. A few seeds stuck to him. I picked some off his lips and nibbled them. This made him cry again. Apa took him home.

I skipped to the schoolhouse. Mummy was teaching English and first aid to the women. They would repeat everything, their bodies rocking.

"They mimic and mimic but they don't understand. What can I do, Noori?" she asked me as she got up. "But they're so sharp about the dressings and knots."

We left early to help with the feast.

We had fled that summer before the Japanese advance. Amma withdrew us from Bishop Heber, and we said tearful farewells to our classmates. Daddy promised to follow soon. Pandey Uncle, the engineer, and Mr. Maudwell, Daddy's foreman, were to take us to Hla Khine Kyi's village in the hills where his uncle was the headman. Later, Mr. Maudwell told us that Daddy was organizing the escape of several hundred Indians from all over the country. We were to wait here for the right time to join Daddy's group bound for Bengal. It would be safer. Mr. Maudwell returned to the factory after he'd brought us here.

The village was exhilarating. We were free of the tiresome school routine. After a few weeks, we forgot about our friends and school, and started helping Mummy in the fields and with nursing. It was strange to see her, so frail and pale, labouring with the others in the rice paddies under a conical hat. Every day, Hla Khine Kyi and Pandey Uncle would try to dissuade her. They would argue agitatedly with her, but she would straighten up, push a bang back into place, and go on working. Sometimes Apa and I would also go with her. At the end of the day, we would have lime juice ready for her. I was happy to help with the harvest feast.

The women were still bringing in the crops. The men were preparing to roast the pigs by the river. They had stripped to the waist to dig the pits. They fixed the spits, tore off twigs and brush, and slaked the pit mouths with coal. Hla Khine Kyi was among them, clear-cutting the bristles with a blowtorch, pouring hot water on the corpses, scraping the stubble with a metal comb, then sluicing boiling water again. His radio was playing at full volume. The women arrived. The pigs were in place above the lilting flames. They basted the meat, the sauce hissing with impatience into the fire, as two men rotated the spits. There was a flash of blue whenever the salt touched the fire, and you could hear the little pop of mosquitoes that had ventured too close to the flames.

I had seen Hla Khine Kyi and his brothers kill the pigs. They had chased them as they ran round in the pen. When Hla Khine Kyi caught one, he sat on it as if on a horse, pulled up its snout to stifle the noise, and cut its throat while the rest squealed. The others collected the blood in a bucket. After gutting them, they heaved the dead pigs on their shoulders and ran, bobbing with the dead white weight, wearing them like the falls of saris.

The brothers were chased by children, including Thambi, who shrieked with delight, pointing and giggling and pulling a trotter. Warnings were given as they slammed the carcasses on the bench, like dhobi's loads. The heads lolled. You could see the open sternums with glints of ribs, like the ceilings of churches in books. The tails were curled, as if in protest.

The prayers were said and the offerings made. People sat on the grass or on steps. Children played on the verandah. The food came in bowls and pots out of houses. There was fish, chicken, pork, noodles, rice, and papayas, bananas, and mangoes. Everybody was eating and laughing and talking. Some also sang and recited some harvest poems. Hla Khine Kyi was eating and talking with his uncle. They seemed to be arguing. He seemed upset. Then they both got up. The headman went to his hut, and I saw Hla Khine Kyi go to his usual spot under the tree. He drank something from a bottle. After a while, he went to his hut to sleep, as he usually did in the evening. We sat and talked with Pandey Uncle. Mummy looked tired.

It was late evening. The biopic man was here. Some of us crowded around the stand to see the scenes of the Eiffel Tower, Taj Mahal, and London Bridge. Suddenly, everyone was quiet. A shadow had emerged from the trees. It turned into a tall, shambling white man, a redhead with a pencil moustache and an accent that I only later recognized as West Country. He approached our group. He asked for the headman brokenly in some dialect. He introduced himself as Major Crosthwaite. Another man joined him. He was a doctor, the first man said, Dr. Greville. They needed supplies, a radio, and a place to rest. They had some wounded. Mummy offered to interpret. She took them to the headman's hut.

Then the rest came streaming quietly out of the dark. There must have been twenty of them. They had two mules with bamboo panniers full of equipment. They sprawled on the grass in clusters far from us. Most were dressed in brown or khaki with soft broad-brimmed hats. Two or three had their shirts wrapped around their waists, which had made the villagers laugh. One of them planted a flag with a chinte on a blue ground. There were two men in bandages. Most of them seemed as weak as puppies. They kept staring at the food. We guessed who they were. We identified blacks, whites, Nepali, Kachin, Chinese, and Indians.

The comments around us were easy to overhear even if they were whispered. Who were they? Pandey Uncle asked the headman some questions. Why should we help them? They've ruined us, treated us like dogs. Europeans out. Asia for Asians. Mummy reappeared. She asked Apa and me to bring some food and drinks. We took them clay pitchers of water and some sticky rice and lapai jindo, at which the tommies turned up their noses. Pandey Uncle helped to serve but still looked wary.

"'Cor, what a pong. Dead dog, or something," said one from the company.

"Dried shrimp. Quite delicious," said a man, a corporal, "if you can get past the smell."

"Shrimp, Rawlings? This one they make from syphilitic pigs."

"Don't know, Ibby. I'm not a cook like you."

"Fancy a piece of that, though. Eh? Wouldn't mind rooting through her you-know-what."

"Here, you filthy pig, leave off. Randy sod." Some laughter.

"Come on, take a look at that one. Haven't seen such huge behinds in me life. I'd like one with that long neck and that lovely behind. Get in one and yer lost for life, mate."

Someone raised a hand and everyone stopped. There was a noise. Apa pulled me, and we ran with Pandey Uncle to the verandah of the schoolhouse. The soldiers were alert, their tiredness gone. They were lying flat on their stomachs on the ground, their guns trained on the bush. Some started crawling backwards from that position towards the houses. The rustling and cracking noise drew closer, and then he spilled out of the thicket in a heap at the end of the road.

"Christ, it's Solly, the poor bastard. Hang on, lad," Rawlings exclaimed, jumping to his feet.

Rifles lowered, they surrounded the man. One man ran to the hut.

"He's bleeding. Shot in the leg. Bone's out. Where's the doc?"

"Sweet Mary, he dragged himself on that? Check and see if the wood's clear," said their leader.

"I didn't even notice he was gone," Rawlings said.

"Too busy playing with yourself, probably," said Ibbotson.

"Solly, you all right, man?" asked Rawlings.

"Bloody bad manners, Solly. Didn't your mum teach you to hold your liquor? Hold on, son, doc's coming," Ibbotson said.

Their colonel, our bo gyi, and the doctor arrived. Looking down at the stretcher, the doctor spoke:

"He's all right. Lost a lot of blood by the looks of it. I'll have to patch him up, clean up the wound. Pull up his trouser leg, Broome. Cut it. Gently. Christ, look at that. Leeches. Have to get rid of them first. Give me that ciggy, corporal. He needs some morphine. Easy, son. Where's that Indian nurse? Ask her to help me clean this up and splint this, will you, Ibbotson?"

He bore the burning without a word, although his body flinched once or twice. His eyes flickered open to reveal unfocused pale blue irises.

They removed the wounded man on a stretcher. One bloodied arm, glinting white with pale hair, drooped over the side of the litter. Mummy and the doctor started to work on the leg. He signalled weakly for a smoke. Pandey Uncle thrust his own lit cheroot between the wounded man's lips. It left him sputtering and wheezing.

"Sweet fuckin' Jesus. What's this, Abdul, Cuban tar?" asked the doctor, plucking the cheroot from Solly's hand and flinging it away. "Move on, jaldi, jao, jaldi."

Pandey Uncle walked away stiffly.

The colonel told the men to relax. He talked to the headman. He ordered a recce of the village area with two villagers and a scout.

After a while, they brought Solly back to the group. Apa and Mummy went inside. I played with Thambi in the schoolhouse. I looked for Hla Khine Kyi but I could not find him.

Some laughter broke out.

"Come on, Callum, ask him. He won't bite. Come on."

"Nae, nae, I cannae."

"Oh yes, you can. Be a man. Sir, Callum here wants to ask you something."

"Yes, Callum, what is it?"

"Hmm, sair, why's a major like a bottle of red wine?"

"Eh, because we are so rich and mellow. Is that it? No idea. Why?"

An American voice interjected.

"I took this test, see, officer exam, in Ohio. You know, multiple choice, that kind of thing. What's the big deal about that? None of the above. It really got me. Why ask a question if it's none of the above? I mean, why waste a fucking question? None of the above. Come on."

There was some laughter. It subsided.

"I give up, Callum. So why's a major like a bottle of red wine?"

"Because, he's narrow at the top, sair, red in the neck, acid in the middle, and round and boozy in the bottom. No offence, sair."

"Just remember he also packs a kick," he said with a laugh, ruffling the boy's hair. "We'll be out soon. Callum, look after your bugle."

"Yes, sair."

"Here, heard the one about General Will? He was a few ranks higher than Major Obstacle."

I crept closer to the circle of soldiers who had lit a brush fire to keep away the flies. The sharp leaves of the bamboo nearly cut me, and twice I brushed a caterpillar off my blouse and dried leaves from my sarong. I remember it well, that scene.

"Footy season mustav started. Could've been at a Rovers match now. Pints with the lads and then home with the missus and kids. Jesus, I miss that," said Rawlings.

"Never cared for all that. Grown men in short pants running round in circles, booting a fucking ball. What's the bleeding use of that? I ask you. Waste of brass. Are they still playing, war and all? Footy season."

"Too bad it isn't durian season, boys. They say that when the fruit comes down, the sarongs go up," said the one named Ibbotson, crooking his head at me.

I could see them on their haunches, their kits and rifles beside them, their yellow teeth and faces streaked with dirt, and the smell of rancid fat and oil everywhere. The glow-worms had appeared. The evening hissed on and the lanterns were lit.

The wounded man lay on his stretcher. His thigh was in a splint. His right arm lay in plaster like a piece of lagged pipe. He smiled weakly. His eyes flickered and his chest heaved. The burly corporal sat beside him, fanning the flies away and feeding him rice. Some of it dribbled on his shirt front. He gestured when he'd had enough.

"Nice bristols, there. Wouldn't mind polishing my rifle, there. Get it all shipshape in that fashion. Be the pride of the brigade," Ibbotson continued.

"Noori, come here," Mummy's voice called out with perfect timing.

"Hmm, Noori, nice name. That your sister? The older one?"

The man sculpted a huge bosom out of the air. Laughter followed.

"Leave her alone, Ibbotson. For Christ's sake, she's just a child. Don't you talk about anything else? One-track minds, you and the rest."

"Pipe down, pious Patrick Broome. She's old enough. All these village girls, they mature faster. I know, trust me," Ibbotson said.

"Yeah, don't get on your high horse, Father Broome. You Catholics sure breed like rabbits. We all know that," said the American.

Ibbotson turned to the American, made a sign of the cross over him, and intoned Irishly.

"Now, what's this you'd be telling me, sor? You wouldn't be saying that you don't accept Jesus Christ as your lord and saviour, would you now? Do you know god, my son?"

"Sure I do, big woman works at General Electric."

"God's a man, son."

"Is she now?"

Ibbotson continued his mock catechism.

"And Jesus Christ's his son. Are you so ignorant then, you poor, unsaved heathen?"

"His son, no less. That's no bloody use to me. Didn't he have some nieces my age?"

"That's enough from you lot." Broome picked up his kit and walked over to the doctor.

"Can't take a joke, young sourpuss."

"Always said nothing wrong with religion as long as it doesn't get in the way of sinning now and again. Port Said's the place for that. The bints, you know."

"Oh, look, Solly's smiling."

"No rest for the wicked, eh, Solly? Any of these mädchen take your fancy? What, that huge-bottomed one? Ay, 'e's a right lad."

"Ah, son, those are the ways to hell. Fearsome are the trials and torments there, have you not heard tell?"

"Hell? Why should I be afraid of hell? I come from Crawford, Texas."

"Oh, cut that out, Rawlings and you," Broome said as he returned with Dr. Greville to check on Solly.

"Steatopygia. It's natural among the Andamanese and certain tribes here. The fat buttocks help the women survive in these climates. They're a sign of beauty and childbearing, but some of the birthrates here have been falling. Odd. No one knows why."

"Thanks for nothing, Doc. You're spoiling some of the nine wonders of the world for us, you know," said the American.

"Nine? I thought there were seven," said Broome.

"Plus two here."

The doctor sat by the stretcher.

The major returned to the group. He sent Broome to see if the village had any spare ammunition. He squinted to make out the scene, and then took out his pipe. He walked over to the injured man.

"Care for a swig, Berliss? If the good doctor allows."

"Not right now, sir. Not after the injection."

"We got through after all. It's no go, Greville. The Japs are northeast in the caves. They'll probably rest for some time. We blew the bridge over the Shweli. They may cross the chaungs, though, which are full. HQ expects them in a week's time." The major took out his pouch and flicked his head at the headman's hut.

"Nah, the krauts and the nips against us? They don't have a prayer, sir," said Rawlings as he fanned the wounded man. "Not a chance, sir, not half."

"We'll bivouac in the clearing by the temple. A good watershed, forage for the animals, and fruit trees. The bo gyi will send us some food until our supplies arrive. Round everyone up, Rawlings. Keep it quiet. We leave right away before it gets dark. Patrols every two hours. Sentries round the clock. Riflemen Pun and Ibbotson first on the roster. Dhillon and Sarkar, then Amin and Wainwright, Dutt and Hippisley. Got that? Rest for two days. Get some sleep. Up at nine tomorrow. No reveille, just whistles, Callum?" the major said.

The boy nodded.

"Greville, get that Indian nurse to take charge. Berliss and Rawlings can stay with the doctor at the headman's for the time being. Radio still out? Use the headman's radio. It's all right, Rawlings. Secure. Get a message to HQ and reconnect with the brigade. That river crossing was murder. We've got to link up with the rest of the column. Wait here for the confirmation. Get White City to airdrop supplies. Indent us some clothes, post, rations, books, the lot. Where's our runner?"

"Yes, sir. Ours is still on the blink," Sarkar says. "Dhillon thinks it's some valve. Indian chap in the village is an engineer. Thinks he can get it working in a day or two."

"I see. Good. Right, men. Prepare to move. No fraternizing with the locals, Ibbotson."

"Man's got eyes in the back of his head. Spoils all the fun," I heard Ibbotson whisper to Rawlings.

Broome had returned in a rage. He spoke to the major and wandered over to the others.

"That bloody headman or bo gyi or whatever he is won't give us any ammo. Says he needs it to defend his village. He has it. Didn't deny it, even showed me the piles. Quite an armoury. The mammering, mast-fed ponce. We should just take it," Broome said.

"Hey, Broomey, come on over here. Bring your tail, shoot the shit with us."

"I say, he may be a shit but shooting him's a bit drastic, whatever his faults, headman and all that, you know."

There were hoots of laughter.

The wounded man spluttered as the corporal tipped the water canteen a little too quickly.

"Don't choke the boy."

"Sorry, eh, Solly. We'll come visit. No grapes. We promise. Take it easy, lad," said Rawlings.

Four of them carried the man on the stretcher into the hut. The soldiers picked up their gear.

"Callum, a moment," Dr. Greville said.

"Doc?"

"Know anything about sheep earmarks in the Hebrides? Doing a monograph. Finished the one on desert grasses."

"Sheep, sair? City boy, sair, sorry. Glasgow," Callum said.

"Ah."

They came back the next day to shift Solly to the encampment in the jungle. Mummy went with them. Apa and I had to stay with Pandey Uncle for safety. Hla Khine Kyi had disappeared. One of Mummy's students said he had joined the rebels. Four days later, Rawlings burst into the schoolhouse where the headman was talking to Pandey Uncle. He said that a Japanese unit had outflanked them and shelled them in the night. They had managed to get away. Two dead. He wanted to radio for support. I asked him for news of Mummy. He said she was safe but they were going to move soon. She would send for us. He hinted that they'd been betrayed. The headman nodded grimly.

Mummy didn't send for us. She never came.

It's hard to be sure though when the others did. The cowherd who grazed his flocks by the river ran to tell us the Japanese were coming. They marched into the village in strict formation as fresh as the morning. Half of them had bicycles. Captain Honda was polite. He called us one by one into the schoolhouse, and quizzed us about the enemy. Later, they summoned all of us again, including children and old men and women, to the headman's hut. I was surprised to see Pandey Uncle in some kind of army uniform by the captain's side, clearly advising him. The captain looked at his large silver watch and spoke. Pandey Uncle acted as the translator. I hadn't known that he spoke Japanese.

Hla Khine Kyi's brothers were missing. I'd heard the whispers. They were going to join the rebels too. They were going to fight the Japanese and the English, and throw the Indians out as well. The captain, accompanied by Pandey Uncle, moved down the ranks to us. He grimaced as he inspected everyone. When he got to Thambi, he paused. The boy's skin was beaded with fear, but he broke into a huge smile. The captain slowly unhooked his fingers from his belt where he wore his revolver, and chucked him under the chin with a lopsided smile. We relaxed.

Then the captain announced that we had to show up for work at dawn the next day. There would be no exceptions, except infants and bedridden old people. Frightened and confused, we looked at the headman, who kept quiet. He just nodded to us. There was a head count. Before he dismissed us, the captain sent two soldiers to search the village. We waited in the sun. Hla Khine Kyi's brothers were dragged out into the compound by four soldiers. The captain walked over to the men and slapped them hard. The younger brother blinked, but the elder one stood up and leaned over and spat in the captain's face. The soldiers clubbed him to the ground. The captain took off his specs and wiped his face with a handkerchief. The headman looked at the brothers with something like sadness.

We assembled at dawn. We were led to the ditch, all of us, even the headman and Thambi. I remember the silence. Some of us were given panniers, others tools. The strongest were given pickaxes and gear, and the women trowels and scythes for the grass. The men started holing out the debris, which got passed in a line near the ditch. We sheared off the weeds and tangles. The work was tiring with the sun overhead and the dirt sifting through the panniers on to our hair and faces.

The sentries stood sharply at the watch and shouted sometimes. The headman could not work so quickly; he took breaks. Someone usually helped him. Once he stopped to light a cheroot. A soldier who was above him clubbed him on the head, and he fell into the ditch, blood over his face. The sentry yelled to try to stop the men who moved to pick him up, but everyone who had spades, mattocks, and pickaxes advanced in a group. He retreated. He allowed them to lift the old man and put him down in the shade, but kept his rifle levelled at the helpers' midriffs. Later, two soldiers lifted the old man and dragged him back to the village.

In the evening, it was a different sight. Our headman was tied naked to a cross made from beams from the teak yard. His striated flesh hung loosely from his bones. Apa whispered, "Pandey Uncle tells me they found the radio, the ammunition, and some stuff from the wounded soldier who stayed there. I think he told them." They had impaled his arms and legs with bayonets. Then the torture session began, and we were forced to watch. He was probably unconscious through most of it, but they revived him from time to time with slaps and by throwing water on his face. They jabbed and goaded him with bayonets before they pierced his eyeballs. One soldier sliced his testicles and thrust the knife through his penis and up to the sternum, just as Hla Khine Kyi had disembowelled the pigs. The intestines appeared in a steaming heap. People cried silently, not daring to moan or sob. I just hope that he was already dead by this time.

Then the brothers were brought forward. They were naked. Their hands were tied. The older brother's face was puffy and mottled. His teeth were broken. A soldier beat them with bicycle chains until their skins hung in strips. They were quizzed again about the rebels. Who were they? How many? What was their uniform? What arms did they have? When would they attack? Did they wear special badges? What did they carry? Where were they headed? They did not answer. The soldiers brought a bucket of pickling salt and threw it on them. They writhed and screamed. The bayonets went into action. Their bodies, swollen and black, were left outside the headman's hut until the next evening. This was a lesson to us, Apa said.

I asked Apa, didn't Pandey Uncle tell the captain about Mummy? She told me to be quiet. Anyway, I couldn't bring myself to ask him about Mummy when he came by later. He was very solemn. He spoke slowly and gently. Obviously, he had some news, some bad news. Workers had stormed the office when they learned the sugar factory was going to close. Daddy had pulled out a gun and shot one in self-defence. The mob had attacked and killed him in turn. I didn't understand. To me, it seemed like a story. It did not feel real. Apa cried every night and I comforted her. I could not feel anything.

The airstrip was more or less ready after three weeks. There were just about fifteen yards to go. We were working that afternoon when they came shining out of the sun, their angry engines spitting fire. We dived into the ditch, the panniers over our heads, dirt all over us. I clutched Thambi, who trembled and cried. I saw the neat rows of shells stitching up the strip. There were two planes. The soldiers fired at them as they buzzed by. They reloaded before the second strafing run. As the roar of the planes grew and their shadows came, I pulled Thambi and Apa and ran into the jungle. I remember streaking into the bamboo groves past the ditch, with Apa shrieking at me, but I don't remember any bombs.

When we returned, we found that a villager had died and one had been hit in the leg and shoulder. This was the only time the planes came to the village that I remember.

The airstrip was completed but it didn't seem to be used. We didn't have to do any more labour. The village returned to its earlier rhythm, but we now served the captain. There was no headman.

&

I was skipping through the house compound, coming back for lunch after picking fruit on a hot day. I saw the soldiers in their hut eating their rice. They waved at me. I waved back. It was odd. The house was still and dark. Usually, at this time, she would be on the verandah, washing out the dishes. Where was Apa? I couldn't hear anything.

Before I walked into the room I shared with her, I remember pausing to draw a face in the dust on the windowpane. Calling out "Apa, Apa," I walked, trailing my fingers on the furniture. Her door was ajar but something in the atmosphere froze, and I felt uneasy.

"Apa?" I called. I smelled sweat and rice liquor in her room. As I leaned over her bed and moved the mosquito net aside, a hand with a silver watch appeared and suddenly gripped mine. I heard her shout "let her go" and the slurred reply, but the grip tightened. There was a struggle. Then I saw a flashing arc of something hard and sharp and silver, heard the thud and the gurgle, and then he was still and I was free. I opened my mouth to scream. This time, I felt her hand cover my mouth.

"Be quiet. It's all right, it's all right. Don't scream, Noori, whatever you do, don't scream. For god's sake, don't scream. Ssshhh."

Bewildered, my mouth open in a soundless O, I shook her off and ran silently through the open door, a sticky warmth spreading between my legs. When I rushed out, blinded by the glow of the evening, I saw a growing patch of red on my lungi. I raced past the schoolhouse down the path that ran parallel to the ditch and the airstrip. Here I was, moving through the bamboo groves, my slippers gone, my breath coming in clumps. Trees flashed by like spectres, blurred by my tears, distorted by my breathing. I tripped on something and landed with a thump and a whimper. I picked up a bamboo stick, which I waved blindly in front of me to clear a way.

I paused to thrust my hand between my legs. It came away covered in blood, with a stink of iron. My thighs were gluey and my stomach weak and bloated, and I felt I was draining out of life fast. Now I was screaming as I got up again and grabbed the bamboo, running once more. I tore towards the river. The saal trees appeared. My tears came in a barrage. A fist clutched my heart. I was dying. The grass was wet under my feet, and there was dark mud squelching through my toes. I ran and stumbled.

I was not far from the river, but I wanted to reach it quickly, lose all my traces, heal myself, but as I ran, the earth turned slithery under my feet. I slipped and skidded on something rubbery and pliable and alive but kept going until I looked down and saw the hundreds of snakes that I was running on in my bare feet, snakes the colour of grass that were twinning slowly, winding in and out of their embraces, their glitter reddening with the dying sun, a slowly undulating carpet, tamped and trampled, the warp and woof moving sadly, endlessly, in a weave through the rituals of life and birth with half-open eyes filmed with desire. There were thousands, all round, copulating on the banks as far as I could see. I thrashed about in a frenzy. Some stopped moving or uncoupled, and tried to move away when they felt my force. Others slowed down as the bamboo descended; on some, ruptures appeared, slow glistenings oozing out of the wounds.

I flailed away for god knows how long, whimpering and crying until they found me, Apa with Thambi in her arms, and we went into the river and then climbed up and ran deeper into the jungle. How long we ran before we stopped, I don't remember. We raced along a dirt track past a mound in the jungle that I no longer knew, my sister and I. She was holding my hand and carrying Thambi. Apa looked at me and dragged me whenever I stopped so that I nearly cried out and fell. Where was Mummy? I wanted Mummy. I was crying for her. Thambi never cried. Perhaps he recalled another flight, a greater horror. Apa cleaned me with soothing noises and inserted a rag to stop the bleeding. She said Mummy had gone away but Pandey Uncle had said we could find her, maybe.

The forest was endless, productive, alive. We penetrated the dark womb of the jungle, feeling safe. The calling of the animals did not frighten us; even the crashing shape of an elephant breaking cover and trumpeting by made us more resolved to get in deeper. It was towards morning that we found Hla Khine Kyi in charge of his rebel camp. He had already heard about his brothers and showed us a photograph of the family that he always carried. We rested and talked while his radio played and his men stood on guard. He said we had to move quickly. They would search the forest. The village had probably been razed already, he suspected, the men killed. He would escort us with some men to the road that would take us to India.

I don't remember much about this march except that we climbed into the interior heading towards the sunrises and that it took four or five days, maybe longer. He told us stories while we walked, but I could see his heart was not in them. He left us on the day that we met the stragglers. He stopped and opened his tunic pocket. He gave me the photograph, and then he and his men turned and left. I never saw him again.

My pocket was full of miriams that I had picked in the forest, and I shared them with the others who were on the move: Palaungs, Erchis, Karins, Shans, Bengalis, Gujaratis, Biharis, English, and Tamils. There was a cart laden with furniture, including a Kienzle grandfather clock with a cracked crystal, which chimed every quarter hour. It stuck out between the shafts of the cart, the greased wheels and pins bending under its weight. We got on in turns. Other families walked by, children on the shoulders or on cycles, their belongings strapped to a pole or bundled; some without anything. Occasionally, orphans would cry for their mothers, or the madwoman, suspicious of everyone, would scream at the wind.

Finally, we saw that Indian family from the Ramlila, the four girls and some boys. And we ran with their gharry for a while. The man saw us and put us in the car. Farther up, we found Mr. Maudwell walking with some traders. We pumped him for news, but he was withdrawn and would not say much. He was upset about Daddy. He said he hoped they would hang Pandey. He said he was a traitor like the rest of Bose's crew. I didn't know what he meant.

The food for the animals was running out, and it was hard to make them go. We started coming across corpses: refugees shot, one with his head blown off and maggots feeding, a baby in swaddling clothes, abandoned, starved, dead, half-eaten by dogs. All talk was stilled. We creaked along in silence. We could feel them.

A Japanese convoy came flying past. Their soldiers opened fire but kept going. Everyone ducked or ran. We stopped the gharry after the noise of their engines had long faded. I went looking for them. Apa had fallen on the road but she was unharmed. I saw him, Thambi, hit by a bullet and then crushed under the wheel of the cart with the clock, which had overturned. We stopped to bury him.

Then the rains fell in sheets for days. Winged ants appeared in the evening, bumping into the lanterns and burrowing through the food, pismires all over the sweetmeats, all the way till we reached the border. We found our way to their shelter, and then we went to the cantonment where, mercifully, they had news.

WHITENESS

What, did you think that once you saw it everything would become clear, that it would be so easy to decipher? Like bits of coloured glass in a tube that fall into a pattern when shaken, a pattern that you could recognize? Did you expect to see the images develop on paper out of nothing? Images, nothing but images without sense. Through the airplane window, you saw the sea of clouds seamed with red. You thought how you would have described this once: a field of cotton on fire, the sun a red-necked overseer—a wound on the horizon. There it was, in the break of the clouds: the temples scattered on the plain like rubies in a palm and the hills in the dark guarding them like knuckles. More images without a story.

Then, of course, your doubts. You couldn't even be sure you had seen it before, in some documentary. Or had you really walked here? You knew that if you put your thumb across the pane like a child you could block out everything. No sun, no clouds, no plains, no plane, no pain. But remember what they had said? *Accept everything, admit everything, deny nothing. Do things by rote and it will all return. Everything will come. One day.* No doubt you felt a bit queasy too, like a girl before her exams. You couldn't deny the warm patch of comfort spreading in the stomach or the itch between your legs.

"What do they do? Cut their legs off before they board? These seats are for dwarves." He rattled the tray and pushed the red button alternately. "Christ, I need a piss."

You knew who he was supposed to be but you were never quite sure. *There are only some truths. Stick to them*, the men and women in the white coats had said. Other phrases flitted through your head. *The moon a whitening scar in the pain of the night. And the overweening evening.* Suddenly, you remembered the heft of the Arriflex. Did your shoulder spasm at the memory? They had come easily to you once, all these things that were now denied you. *Why don't you say something? Why are you quiet?*

"Stewardess, my tray is stuck. *Stewardess.* Damn it, Rookie, she's gone. I'll explode...do a Brahe."

You massaged your neck and shoulders. Somehow, you knew that you did this whenever you didn't want to be drawn. You realized without looking that his face was congested, the dewlaps working with anger. His tongue would be passing over his lips as it usually did before an outburst. Then he would bare his teeth in a yellow grimace. It must have been easy to sense the finger running under the collar, exposing a patch of sweat under the arms and the band of wet around the waist that bulged over the seat-belt buckle.

"That bloody woman. Just deaf, or do they all wear earplugs, do you think? *Rookie.*"

The seat-belt sign pinged on. Nervously, your fingers traced the heads of the intertwined snakes on the silver bracelet as if for assurance. Caduceus, heal me. Was that your prayer?

"We're almost there. Another ten minutes or so, hold on," you said in a low voice, as if you were afraid to be overheard.

"Damn it, Rookie. It's bad enough as it is but must you always needle me with your reasonable voice? Why did you suggest this airline? I should have known. Just slip in the old knife. Stick it to old Michael. Why not? Everybody does."

What had he whispered to you about the monk's prophecy after you had beaten the gong at the pagoda before everyone fled to the hills? Telling you all your own stories in hospital as if to a child. He'd enjoyed that. You could tell. What was it? Try. Ah, that it was ordained that you would return. Some such nonsense. So then what were the certitudes? You were at least sure you would know the smell—the air with its hint of salt, fish, and oil, the ripeness of the date palms, and the waft of oris water from the biryani cart. Remembered or imagined?

You worked the knot at the base of the spine with your fingers as he rapped the seat in front. The woman turned around to say sorry, and clicked her seat upright. Her companion, a man of fifty, floated his apology back to you. You nodded.

The purser stopped by your row. He clucked his disapproval, cancelled the light, and put the tray up with a snap. That set him muttering as you knew it would.

"Bloody hell, not flying this outfit again. Never been so uncomfortable. And the service. What service? Damn, can't smoke now. And the air-conditioning... I swear. Fluid dripping down. Who owns this tub, for fuck's sake? It's not airworthy."

He subsided only when the voice announced that you would land soon. You put your hands over your ears to block the rush as the plane braked to a halt, its tires screeching on the tarmac. Finally, it taxied and stopped. Some people clapped, the sound of firecrackers.

You debouched into the stale heat of the evening. The air was still. It smelled of tar and fuel. A queue formed. Army officers with swagger sticks guided the passengers along. Like a parade. He looked cowed. He carried his shoulder bag, muttering to himself, looking for a bathroom. You tried not to notice. The itch was worse.

The uniformed officer stood under the picture of a pink-cheeked general who wore thick, round-framed glasses.

He spoke in an Australian accent as he thumbed through the documents.

"Ah, British, Hippisley. Back from the old country?" he asked slowly. The last phrase was dipped in caustic. Why are interrogation rooms always so bare, so blank? you wondered.

"Are you married? Are you sure? Well, these days you never know. Hmm, it says that your wife was born here, I see."

He glanced sharply at the passport and then spoke rapidly in the language you had sworn you'd never speak again, even if you remembered it.

"Are you Indian? South Indian? Do you know anyone here? Where are you staying?"

You hesitated, then replied in English.

"I've forgotten most of it. I wasn't born here. I've never been here."

"Where are you going?"

"We'll be staying at..." You named the hotel.

"Do you have reservations? Show me." You handed them over.

With him, it was even more brusque.

"Any alcohol? Pornography? Books? How much money do you have? Show me."

Michael handed him everything, including the museum letter.

"What's this?" asked the official.

He examined it and gave it back, but confiscated the guidebook and the duty-free Laphroaig. Poor Michael. He looked ready to protest, a child deprived of his toys, but he was trammelled by his respect—you almost said, fear—of uniforms. Be afraid of the monitor. Manners makyth man. Old public school mottoes.

After a slight pause, the stamp stabbed the passports twice, pressing hard. *Like an eagle claiming a lark.* Again, those images. The epauletted arm waved you two out of the hall. Michael collected the documents. Near the luggage carousel, you saw them, from the row in front. She was about twenty-five. She was clutching her companion's arm as they talked. Her glossy black hair and wispy sideburns reminded you of the women in shalwars in Southall. In spite of the flight, she looked fresh and clear-eyed in her bright cotton T-shirt and jeans. You talked.

Pilar was originally from Puerto Rico. Her husband, Ezekiel Jacob, was a Characin Jew from Bombay who owned a jewellery store in Palo Alto. You admired their casual ease with strangers, so American. The man was slim with a touch of grey about the temples. His beige bush shirt and pleated trousers were creased and damp. You introduced Michael, who offered them a lift when he found that they were staying at the same hotel. A sleepy official waved you all through the final customs checkpoint, right? Tell me if I am wrong. Go on, you can. I'm not infallible. Hardly that.

So how did you all fit into the small Fiat that Htin Aung Kyi had sent? The driver was a stocky, middle-aged man in white with a red bandanna, who drove with his elbow jutting out of the window. He smoked and turned up the radio orchestra. Pilar had fallen asleep, and her head lolled on your shoulder. What was this wave of feeling that made your breasts swell? Why did you feel weepy and want to stroke her head? I hope you'll forgive me for asking. Smoke, the smell of exhaust and sulphur streamed in. Michael peered into the night and asked for the air-conditioning to be turned up. The driver scrolled the windows shut.

"Hot," said Michael.

"Okay."

"What's your name?" asked Michael.

"Ba Leik Sin."

You fell asleep, but the stiffness in your neck kept waking you up. You heard Michael quiz the driver about the museum. The driver was yours for the rest of the stay, Michael whispered over his shoulder. It sounded as if his anger was forgotten.

The hotel was a colonial building with a driveway sweeping to a portico. You could see earlier scenes, imagined or real, sung or spoken, with servants in stiff, starched quiffs with trays of drinks for the drivers of jalopies parked there and riders in jodhpurs on horses that flicked their tails. In your hypnagogic state, you noticed the green shutters.

When he went to look after the bookings, you sat on that unstuffed sofa in the foyer. Why did everything look as if you were gazing through the wrong end of a telescope: the vast lobby with black and white marble tiles, some cracked; the huge fronds in pots near flyblown windows, which reminded you of a station somewhere, was it Spain? You decided that you would ask Michael. Then you saw him relieving the old man who was struggling with your bags. The man bowed with folded hands and muttered his thanks. It was time to get up. The Americans were still with the desk clerk as you went up the stairs.

The room was spacious. You opened the window to get rid of the mustiness and the gluey air that enveloped you. You flopped on the bed. He emerged in the gloom from the bathroom with a towel around his midriff and wanted to lie down. You were too tired to move to let him.

"All right?"

"Back. Bed's too soft." You sat up to pick up the water jug that was covered with a beaded muslin doily and poured. Sodden, that smell of the first monsoon shower when the parched earth gives up its essence.

"You know, Rookie, they say that you get back problems if you do too little, not too much. Look at my father. Hard drill all his life, now goes out and chops wood every day. Not a twinge and he's not young. I know the accident and all that, but it's been months. Maybe the back's a blind. Maybe it's nothing."

Annoyed without knowing why, you knew that he was concealing something. So this was the homecoming. You felt as flat as the water. You were too tired to respond.

Suddenly, the lights went out.

"Oh, Christ, what now? One thing after the other."

"Just a power outage. Hand me the painkillers. They're in my bag. Thanks." You put the glass down.

"That's it. Pop a pill. The cure-all. Where is it? I can't see. Here. Water with that? What's that? A lungi? Looks Scottish. Never wore that. How does one?"

You were silent. Silences always upset him. He tried to please.

"You know, didn't think that Pilar woman would speak English that well. Odd name. I thought she would be like that Mexican teen we met in Málaga. 'Please, my luggages. She is lost.' And our host there who spoke beautiful English most of the time except that morning—you know, when we saw the Alcazar—'How are you from? Who is your name? Why is your job?' Remember? And that funny young girl at the posada who kept apologizing, 'Excuse but my English is not well,' and that Finnish woman who talked about the 'myramids' in Egypt. Surely, you must remember them. What a riot."

You wished he would shut up. You felt like a little girl tickled by the hairy fingers of an uncle who stank of cigars. Something flared like hope in you. Was it something? Your exultation was brief. Nothing else. Another blank, another cul-de-sac, another wall of ice.

There was a soft knock on the door. Michael tightened his towel.

"Enter."

The maid came in with a lantern and placed it on the bedside table.

"How...long...light...gone?" asked Michael slowly.

The maid looked up at him, giggled with her hand in front of her mouth, and pattered out, struggling to close the heavy door.

"Well, that was useful."

"God, don't feel well. Think I'm going to vomit."

He helped you to the bathroom with a look of concern, cupping your elbow in his right hand and holding the lantern in the other. The lamp cast shadows on the shutters as you walked. For some reason, the shapes reminded you of ancient, childish terrors, and even in this state you smiled.

"There's a threshold, mind." He spoke in almost a whisper.

You gripped the sink and retched drily a few times. The belly was tight and hurting.

"Want some lemon juice? I'll get some. Settles the stomach."

You nodded, anxious to be alone.

You waited in the flickering light, your mind skirting the edges of memory. The few images flashed again as they did every evening. Those sepia forms you had seen in your childhood photos: the biopic on its tripod like an insect with its five eyes black like flies, or that walk in the woods, the jackfruit thrown into the river for the dogs to retrieve, the tracery of lace on a blouse, the whiff of jasmine. Is that all it took to make up who one is? Where was the thread that would make it cohere? How do you find your story, your history? Who writes it for you? Was there nothing that you could cut or frame or recuperate? How much truth, how little artifice, how little sense. Shake, shake, shake. Roll the dice.

You had an image of the past summer, of squat eateries along the paseo, the walks on Pedregalejo, and the nausea that the waters always induced in you. Then you remembered the painted pictures on the zoetrope that you had built from a shoebox and threaded spools for the malagueñitos. Pasted images of Manolete's pas de suerte, Picasso's minotaurs in the cave hoping for their doomed escapes, and their favourites—the Mirós.

Another. He was beached like a whale against the pillows backed on the headboard. His penis lay on his right thigh like a thick, white slug oozing smegma. As his faraway look had demanded, you had taken the turkey-dead, stippled, veiny flesh in your mouth where it had probed as you had curtsied and bobbed, and that smell of ammonia that invaded every part of you as you gagged.

You vomited twice.

He was back.

"I checked. There's no food. Restaurants are all closed. Was it the chicken? Must've been," he said when he returned carrying a glass. "I just had the veggies but I swear the strawberry deflated when I pricked it with the fork. It actually hissed. That airline...Okay?"

Nodding, you moved towards the bed. He wiped your brow gently.

"Could be the heat too, you know. Odd, your forehead isn't hot. It's freezing. Maybe dehydration. Drink some more water. Drink lots, okay? Need electrolytes. This has some. Tastes okay, too, eh? Call a doctor?"

"No, just tired. Sleep. I want to sleep."

"You cold? But I want the fan. Damn. Power's out, I forgot. Drink up, drink up. Good for you."

You felt seared with the discomfort and emptiness.

"Why am I here? Who are you really?"

"Oh darling, don't be like that. It'll all come back. Remember what the doctor said? Just give it time. Be patient. Come, lie down. Here, take my arm."

"Tell me why," you whined, hating yourself and the tone of your voice, "why do you love me? Why? Why do you only love me when I am sick or sad? Tell me."

He looked alarmed, almost guilty.

He peeled the green bedspread and squealed when a dead cockroach fell out. For the next ten minutes, he scoured the bed before plumping the pillows for you. The heat clung to you like another skin. Images drifted in and out in an andante, a stately procession of portraits saying and doing odd things in weird settings. You saw a moon through the window. You thought of a mouldering round of cheese.

Just before the fan started whirring and the lights switched on, you saw yourself in another hotel. Where was it? You had woken up in the dark to see the woman kneeling on her bed. You'd gone taut. Then you had realized that she was praying. You remembered that you had met him the next day near the potted palms at the station. He was sweating in his old Burberry. You changed hotels. You knew that it was a dream. Ashamed and comforted, you fell asleep again even before he'd switched the lights off.

✦

The sun dispelled the doubts and shades. Michael was fully dressed in bed, reading his papers. Over a breakfast of fresh bread, fruit, soup, and tea on the verandah, they chatted with the Jacobs, but she still felt weak and drained. When Michael went for a walk, she returned to the room and rested with an Orwell from the hotel library, but the words kept breaking off from their lines and slipping away.

Later in the afternoon, Michael rallied her to go to the bazaar. Ba Leik greeted her warmly as he opened the car door and she got in. The car started and the world spun as if in a slow-motion reel, which she watched from some distance. The car wound its way through the durian and mango stalls, past the dried-fish heaps at the market whose smells pursued them even as they had passed the lum workers. Then they came to the small shop run by an Indian couple. Michael bought a chinlone cane ball, an aingyi, and some food packets for the hotel.

"You never know. Let's go somewhere. To the mountain?"

She nodded, her mind still spinning from the impressions.

"Today...radio phut," said the driver.

"Ah, radio phut today. That's okay, nice day," said Michael.

"Yes, nice day. Sorry, my English not so good. Fourth standard. Old temple, okay, old temple?"

"Ah."

The wind was mummifying. She felt cocooned in its warmth. The drive through the town and countryside took over an hour. When she opened her eyes, the mountain was upon them, all dark crags and shining temples. She took Michael's hand, and she walked with rubbery steps to the crown and the pagodas. They savoured the cool, thin air as they stood between monks with their thabeiks full of flowers or food and their prayer wheels pointing across to the temple plain. This was a moment of serenity. By the time they had walked for an hour, the ground grew too hot. They were ready to leave.

At the hotel, they unpacked the preserves and sauces. She offered him some balanchow for the main course. He scooped up a spoonful into his mouth, crinkled his nose, and chewed very slowly. He gulped the food midway, made a face, and drained a large glass of water.

"Can't see this going down too well at high table," he said.

Something shifted in her mental furniture, the tableau of a pale hand piling pickles and vegetables in the centre of a chapatti on a plate before picking up a knife and fork. She laughed.

"Well, you have it with other stuff."

"Oh, you sound better. The drive did you some good. I'm so glad."

They were on the verandah. Ezekiel and Pilar came in dusty and sweaty.

"The tea here is so strong it gives opinions, as we say back home," said Pilar, pouring her a cup with a laugh. "We went to a bar afterwards."

"We've been with officials all day," Ezekiel explained. "We want to see some mines, maybe import some gems, rubies, sapphires. Nobody shows up on time. Met three, running from office to office. You really need an interpreter. It is difficult to know what they think. All those forms."

"And that traffic. Everyone's in a hurry to be late, Izzy says. That's good, isn't it? They've asked us to come again tomorrow. We want to buy some food, maybe fruit too, now before everything closes. What's a good place? Izzy, tell me, why wouldn't you walk me to the taxi?" Pilar asked.

"You white women are so demanding."

"What's wrong with walking me to the taxi? What sort of a man are you?"

"Because I saw your father at the strip joint."

"It was a bar in the hotel, not a strip joint. He wasn't my father. Don't talk about my father like that," she said with a skipping laugh.

"'Cause he was your father."

"He was a minister. I'm never going out with you again," she said, her eyes merry.

They discussed plans to visit the temples together.

While he massaged her back, he reminded her about dinner at Htin Aung Kyi's at eight. After a shower, she sat on the verandah and read. When she got bored, she watched the maid's daughters play hopscotch in the dirt. She had dressed casually but Michael was sweating in a jacket and tie. Thank God, he hadn't brought a sola topee as he had threatened to do in England.

The drive took them past the market. She fancied that she had begun to spot the landmarks. She felt happy. After half an hour, the car turned into a driveway lined with casuarina trees. The hosts were waiting on the porch. Htin Aung Kyi was a small, neat man with black eyes and a straggly moustache. He wore a green and magenta lungi. He was effusive with his welcome. The family was formally dressed.

"What a pleasure it is to see you, Dr. Hippisley," Htin Aung Kyi greeted them. "Ma Lin, my wife. She's there with our daughter. She's coming. Did you have a good flight? I hope you have found the car useful. We didn't want to disturb you at the hotel. Is it satisfactory? We don't get many books at the museum now but we have yours on the inscriptions. I hope you will have time to give a talk. And you, dear lady, how are you? I believe you are not a stranger to these parts. I believe your family is related to U Rashid?"

"No, I don't think so. I know the name but I don't have any memories of meeting him," she said cautiously. "Thank you for the car. It was very kind."

"Ah, come inside. Ma Lin, maybe you can take the lady through a tour of the garden. My wife."

"Oh, I'd like to see that as well," said Michael.

"Of course. Forgive me, I have to go in for just a minute."

Ma Lin, slim, graceful, came forward with her daughter to lead them through the garden. She had grown up in the capital, the daughter of a general, and had moved here ten years ago, she said. She watched indulgently as her little girl took slim brown pods from her pocket and dropped them into the stream where they crackled and burst open upon contact. The child clapped her hands and grabbed Michael by the edge of the jacket and led him towards the roses near the bamboo bridge. Her pigtails bounced.

Ma Lin asked her if she had done any shopping. She was surprised when she heard that she hadn't seen any lacquer or teak in the market. She offered to take her to some shops. She introduced her to a couple near the verandah. Hkun Pan Sing, who managed a tapioca mill, was from the north. He looked fat and jolly. His wife, a pediatrician, was a hard-faced woman but she spoke gently. There was a tall, erect man who wore a frock coat, English in cut and style. Ma Lin introduced him as Sao On Kya. He spoke in a clipped tone, smoked bidis with a cupped hand, and often consulted his watch that he wore with the dial on the inside of the wrist.

They went in. The house was a large, rambling affair. There were mouldering elk heads on the walls, and old sepia-coloured snapshots and a stool made from an elephant's foot. A folding ivory screen cordoned off the teak dining table from the sitting area.

"What a beautiful house."

"Oh, do you think so?" said Ma Lin. "That's very kind."

"It's the old collector's residence. A Mr. Edward Chandler had it built a hundred years ago. A big-game hunter too," said Htin Aung Kyi as he rejoined the group.

"Now put to much better use, you'll agree," Hkun Pan Sing said with a laugh.

"I'm sure the wildlife's better off now." This was Michael.

"I didn't get the 'No umbrellaring' signs on the mountain," she said.

"Ah, that. They were put up to stop visitors using their umbrellas as pointing devices near temples. It's very rude," said the doctor.

"Dates back to the time of the English. How did you like them?" asked Htin Aung Kyi.

"Oh, it was beautiful. The view, but we had to take off our shoes. The ground was burning hot," she said, "but we haven't been to the plains yet."

The conversation turned desultorily to the state of the temples. Sao On Kya looked bored and began talking to the businessman. Side conversations sprang up.

Eventually, she asked the doctor about swimming and beaches. The Irrawaddy was too swift for swimming, she replied. The current takes a few fisherfolk every year, her husband added. Michael looked agitated. How long ago had it been since she swam? Not since the accident; the physio lessons in the water didn't count. Hkun Pan Sing recounted that he had learned to swim when his grandmother had thrown him down a well. He had been six. He laughed.

Michael said, "Oh, she had no right to do that" and asked him if he still swam. No, he said, but it was a village in which you depended on the river for everything. Being able to swim had saved his life during a tsunami.

"Still, it must be a factor in your life. The trauma, I can only imagine."

"Less a factor now than a fact but a rather interesting one, you must admit. My wife thinks it's just as well that they live abroad, otherwise I might've used that method on my grandchildren."

His wife nodded. "I didn't allow him to teach my son swimming."

Hkun Pan Sing laughed uproariously.

She felt sick.

Michael was grateful for the decanter.

"They took my scotch at customs. I expected some decent malt on such a long flight. That swill, so sweet, what was it? It was too late to pour it back into the goat, anyway."

The hosts laughed. Hkun Pan Sing said it was probably Indian whiskey brewed from molasses.

"Is this too hot for you?"

"Oh no, I love the heat," Michael said as he played with the child.

Then Htin Aung Kyi started reminiscing about his days in the bedsit on Portland Street.

"Those shilling meters," he laughed. "Never been so cold and miserable in my life. Used to sit at the kitchen table near the stove all wrapped in a muffler with Mrs. Nesbitt's pot mitts on to keep warm. Tell me, how is Covent Garden? Has it changed much?"

They talked a little bit about London and their families.

Htin Aung Kyi asked about other guests at the hotel. She mentioned the Indian and Spanish couple. He nodded with cautious approval but looked at Sao On Kya.

"There are Jews in the capital still and some Muslims left in the Arakan," said the doctor in a tone that puzzled her.

Sao On Kya said that in some villages children are still taught that Jews are dirty, smelly creatures.

"How awful." She was horrified. Michael looked uncomfortable.

"We don't get hippies that much now but some of these people who come for boys and girls. Germans, Israelis, Japanese, Belgians, Canadians, Swiss, with big cameras. Some come in groups. Some even with their wives who don't suspect a thing."

At the sideboard, the businessman offered Michael a Partagas from a small velvet-lined humidor, "brought over from Havana by the Castrati," he said with a whispered laugh.

Htin Aung Kyi offered "cheroots, Black and Whites, or 555s. We still get them." Ma Lin lit up a green cigarette.

They talked about the decline. The teak trade was dying, and the tourist boycott meant higher prices for those who did visit. Putting his cigar down, Hkun Pan Sing said what the country needed was a modernization program with investments to bring about sustainable change at the community level and to develop the infrastructure. His wife spoke briefly about farming, which was moribund, and of the hardships on people. Unfortunately, there were troubles in different parts, including the borders. Arms were being smuggled to rebels in an effort to destabilize the country and make it ripe for foreigners to exploit.

"They've stolen our history. They pillaged the temples for statues and murals, and carted them off to Europe. Thomann sold them to the Hamburg Ethnographical Museum. Then it was the opium profits, rice and teak to England. And the Indians took what they could too. It's our gas next. Now they come and preach to us about democracy and human rights, and send their missionaries to convert the poor. What hypocrisy," said Sao On Kya.

"What about people like Luce?" Michael asked. "Surely, he wasn't like that."

"Ah, yes, Luce our saviour. He was certainly better. He just took one of our women," said the doctor with a laugh.

The gong went for dinner. She breathed a sigh of relief. Ma Lin went to put her daughter to bed.

She had not expected this conversation. She felt drained. Dinner was a quieter affair but with new tensions. Michael politely declined the ngapi but showed signs of enjoying the mohinga and the fermented-tea salad. He used his knife and fork to eat the chow chow. At the end, the conversation turned to epigraphy. Htin Aung Kyi said Michael's was the most important contribution to epigraphy since Blagden and Than Tun. Michael flushed and said he was thinking of visiting the museum the next day.

He asked after Professor Po. He had written him about Desrolliers's recension of Mons funerary epigraphs. After two brief exchanges, fourteen months ago, he'd heard nothing. He had written again. One letter had been returned. Was he ill? He'd like to meet him.

A silence fell. The women got up and began busying themselves with the tea.

Htin Aung Kyi spoke deliberately after some hesitation. "There were rumours of some sickness. Po had started behaving oddly, staring at his hands, talking to himself, missing meetings. He changed his work hours at the museum, but that was not unusual. He'd asked if he could for health reasons. I said all right. He began work in the evening after everyone had gone home and finished in the morning."

Hkun Pan Sing said Po had consulted his wife about a medical problem.

"He looked quite pale when I saw him," the doctor confirmed. "I wanted to run some tests the next day to make sure, but he didn't show up. I asked Htin Aung Kyi about him, but he had stopped coming to the museum by then. His wife had also stopped meeting people. They stayed home. Everyone shunned them. Then both husband and wife disappeared. They left behind everything: money, passports, jewels, personal papers, all his research. This was some time ago. They were never found. His sister-in-law lives there now but refuses to see anyone. A real mystery. No, they didn't have children."

"There were all kinds of speculations among the villagers. You know how people talk, but I'm not sure what's true," said Hkun Pan Sing.

"Well, the story is that his wife was a prostitute before she became a nurse, but that might just be gossip. Nobody liked her much. They are both Chinese, you know," said Htin Aung Kyi.

Again, she felt as if the truth was not being told.

The child had reappeared with Ma Lin, who brought the tea. Ma Lin said she couldn't sleep as she was too excited and wanted to be with everyone. Ma Lin put on some music. As the adults clapped out the time, the girl danced to "La Cucaracha." In the middle of "Yes! We Have No Bananas," she stumbled and fell and cut her knee and started crying. Ma Lin hushed her, took her by the hand, and led her away.

In Ma Lin's absence, she offered to serve the tea and was surprised at the weight of the silver teapot. The conversation was in a lull. The evening was over. Ma Lin returned after the child had fallen asleep.

Sao On Kya promised to take care of any complications that might arise during their stay. Htin Aung Kyi insisted on their temple visit the next day. He had waved away the concerns about the other couple.

"Bring them. You'll have two cars. One for you and one for the Americans. And a guide. Best to get an early start before it gets hot. I'll send them at seven. Come to the museum after that."

They thanked him. Sao On Kya went out with him and spoke to Ba Leik.

The "sleep wells" and "thank yous" drifted for a bit.

In the car, Michael asked guardedly, sotto voce, "Rather nice of him. Do you think...?"

"Well connected on both sides."

"Certainly does well out of the museum."

"I liked the wife."

"Didn't seem to care too much for..."

"No, didn't mask that, did they?"

"We should pack a hamper. Get a thermos full of tea also. What do you think?"

"Good idea. No idea what they have out there."

"My book had said not much. Too bad they took it."

The morning arrived sooner than they thought. A car honked twice.

"It's here. It's Ba Leik. It's not even seven yet. Got the food?" she asked.

"Put a jacket on. It'll be cool."

They were a little surprised to find Sao On Kya waiting for them with the Jacobs. The Americans went in the jeep with the guide. Ba Leik beeped his way through the pedal cabs, cycles, and jitneys in the market. The noise and cries of the fishermen, as they lay their catch in the early morning sun, stirred something.

"Market day," said Sao On Kya.

"Oh, look," she said, "eels. Huge ones. Remoras? Morays?"

A policeman raised his hand. The car stopped. Sao On Kya rolled down the window and chatted with the policeman. Onlookers moved away and stared quietly from under the awnings. A motorcade rolled by. First came the two motorcycles, followed by three jeeps, then half a dozen lorries. In one lorry in the middle of the convoy, soldiers were guarding some dirt-stained men and young boys in tattered uniforms. Other infantry sat in the other lorries, their rifles ready.

"Who is it?" she asked.

"Maybe General going to Kamaing mines or maybe trouble in east, brown zone," said the driver cheerfully.

"Why doesn't he fly? Wouldn't that be quicker?" asked Michael thoughtlessly. There wasn't any answer. In response, Sao On Kya snapped at Ba Leik who drove in sullen silence for the rest of the trip.

The noise of the crowd grew. They sped ahead to the plain and waited in the shade for the Jacobs, who dismounted from their jeep a little dusty but animated. The guide had been telling them the most extraordinary stories, Pilar said, about Queen Thaw and silk bags and elephants. She wondered how much of it was true. Michael started to lecture as they walked.

They began the tour at the western edge. Rounding the bend, the temples sprang into view. Pilar drew a sharp breath.

"Oh, so many. I didn't think there would be so many."

"Beautiful from the air, and from here," said Michael.

Michael fashioned a head covering by tying the ends of his handkerchief. He stepped out with the guide. The rest followed. Ezekiel and Pilar stopped to load their cameras, their arms snaking through each other's in happy intimacy like an Indian god's. Suddenly, she looked at Michael with a pang and realized how dead she was, how dead everything was. Sao On Kya stood apart. He was filing his nails. Ba Leik stood close to him, whispering. He seemed to be pleading or apologizing.

Pilar and Ezekiel walked all round the central brick pillar in the pytt. The inside was cool.

"The only surviving Hindu temple," said the guide, peering at them through his glasses, "built by King Taunghthugyi before Theravada Buddhism came here."

Michael was studying the pair of headless brick and stucco figures. He began his speech to her in the tone she knew well, part loving, part exhortatory, but she knew it wasn't meant for her. He was bullying the guide.

"It is interesting that a later king, Kyanzittha, styled himself a bodhisattva and claimed transmigrational descent from vishnu, long after Theravada had been established as the ruling religion here. An aberration. There is no shiva temple here though. We should see the sikhara. They used Pyu building techniques particularly near the cella. Maybe Pilar knows something about that."

"A finely carved figure in the museum, though, sir," said the guide.

"Is it back? Wasn't the vishnu anantasayin figure lost?"

"Yes, sir," said the guide. Now he would agree with anything, she knew.

Michael looked pleased.

They had to climb single file past the chintes and nats guarding the steps. Then she saw the huge seated buddha in the dark. Pilar fell in step with her, her hair flying like a prayer flag in the wind that was sweeping across them.

"Can you imagine this place at the height of its glory? The people living here, the colour, the ceremonies?" she asked excitedly.

Some locals were laying flowers and prostrating themselves. From the entrance they could see the two massive blocks of the Thatbyinnyu pagoda piled up like a mountain.

"Care to climb to the top?" Pilar asked.

She declined and sat against the wall and watched the edges of the red-brick mounds sharpen in detail in the sunlight.

"Ah, didn't go with the fifth camcorder regiment from Fort Worth, Texas? Not coming?" Michael asked as he began his climb.

She shook her head.

Ezekiel was the first down with his video camera. Sao On Kya was behind him but moved away. It was obvious that they had been talking. Ezekiel looked uncomfortable and talked fast.

"Great view. Just fabulous. Tough climb but there's a nice breeze up there. Worth every step. You should see it. You can see everything for miles. Top of the world," Ezekiel said.

"Thanks, but I'll stay put. Got a lot of walking and climbing to do yet," she said with a laugh. "Might as well save my strength."

"Beautiful country, this. Food sucks, though. Big time. Pilar can't stand the smell of the chicken. And that fish. Stinks."

Probably because they actually have a smell and taste instead of that plastic that passes for food there, she thought.

Pilar and Michael came down with the guide. Sao On Kya emerged from nowhere with that nail file in his hand. Ba Leik squatted on his haunches in the shade and watched them. Sao On Kya went over to him, and he left for the car.

"What's that that everybody's looking at?"

"Mashaw-tsi or some call it mway kike say. Very rare. Just in flower. Comes in from the north. Many curative properties. Antidote for snakebites," said the guide.

"Hey, wait, Izzy, it looks like the euonymous that the Johnsons have in their sunroom," said Pilar.

"If we ever get bit by a rattler, we'll know where to go, hey hon?" said Ezekiel.

"They're not supposed to sell it here," Sao On Kya interjected.

"Next we visit another temple, similar to the Thatbyinnyu," said the guide, eager to move on.

"Hello, can you take a group photograph before it gets too hot?" she asked. She held out her camera.

They jostled for places. She stood between Michael and Sao On Kya. The Jacobs stood a step above.

They had been walking for two hours. Her legs were tired. She saw the whitewashed façade reflect the sun as she climbed the steps. The guide pointed out that the buddha in the south looked sad or happy, depending on where you were standing. They walked around the figure.

"Oh, it's true," whispered Pilar in a happy tone.

"I can't see it," she said.

"Mira, mira. There, look, the buddha's smiling," Pilar said delightedly, pulling her by the hand. She pronounced it the way Americans say "gouda."

"I still can't see it."

Outside, children were running up the stairs and laughing. The others went to the terrace for the view. The tinkling of the htis came to them from the monks loitering near their huts. After a while, the group walked ahead. Sao On Kya and Michael were deep in conversation.

Michael was taken with the library. He plied the guide with questions that she knew were meant more to impress and intimidate. He probably already knew the answers. The others wanted to see the stone buddha, eroded as it was.

They walked past the kyaungs and another green-tiled temple towards a gateway that led to the spires and crenellations of another pagoda.

Pilar asked her if she had any children.

"One, a girl, studying in the USA."

"How old?"

"Just turned twenty."

"But you are so young. I have two little ones. They are with my mother-in-law, Ezekiel's mother, in LA. I miss them so much. I wanted to bring them but they have school. I want to buy them something special. What do you do?"

Pilar's freshness and energy tired her, but something like an ache developed inside. She tried not to be cynical.

"Film, wow. I'm an architect but Izzy doesn't want me to work in some office. 'Come to the store,' he says. 'You'll be your own boss.' He wants me to be a mother but I get bored at home. I want to build houses. Not big mansions but good houses for ordinary people, good affordable houses."

Pilar had a smut of bronze on her nose. She smiled, reached out, and touched it gently.

"Outrageous."

"Oh, he's not like that. He's generous that way. He gives me money. Oh, there they are. He's waving."

Pilar bounded away. Suddenly, she saw herself as she had looked in the bathroom mirror the first night. Her breasts were fuller, the nipples darker. *Soon, it'll all pass and we'll fade into another age.*

Michael had turned brick red, and his wrinkles were filled with dirt.

"In the afternoon, we'll do some south temples and on Friday we will start from the Shwezigon. How's that?"

Pilar and Ezekiel said they'd have to leave early. They were going to Mogaung in the morning.

From the Bupaya where they spent the longest, she could hear the rush of the Irrawaddy. She watched the boats skim by and heard the shouts of the boatmen coming in for lunch and felt disquieted.

"Sure would be nice to catch the sunset over the river from here," said Ezekiel.

"You'd need a guide. The stairs are not safe in the dark," said Sao On Kya.

"I'd like to hire a boat and spend some time on the river," she said.

"But, darling, you know what the doctor said," Michael said.

Fuck the doctor, she thought with a surge of anger, *and fuck you.*

After Ezekiel and Pilar left for the hotel, Sao On Kya accompanied them to the museum. Htin Aung Kyi offered them refreshments in the office. He introduced them to another colleague. Michael inquired about his research. She wandered slowly through the small building, looking at the exhibits. They hadn't been dusted. She asked Htin Aung Kyi to explain the inscriptions on the pillars that she had seen. He started talking about the Epigraphicas Birmanica and

Indica. She tried to pay attention but felt tired and dizzy and almost fell. Alarmed, Htin Aung Kyi asked if she wanted to eat or drink something, She shook her head. She assured him it was nothing serious, probably just a touch of the sun. He called Michael and suggested that the driver take her back to the hotel. He could carry on in the afternoon as planned, she assured him.

"Do take care, Rookie. Get some rest. I'll see you later."

In the evening, she woke up to find him by her side studying some photostats.

"Better?" he asked.

She nodded.

He put the papers aside. He gave her a stationery set of red and black lacquer. After his circuit, he had gone to the Shwe Leiht Min market that Ma Lin had mentioned. She was quite pleased.

Later, they had the food that Ma Lin had sent. She ventured out to the verandah where they saw the Jacobs. She talked to Pilar about lacquer. She took another shower before she went to bed. The itch was there.

The next day, Michael left for the museum after an early breakfast. He promised to send the car back just in case. She had decided to rest. She still felt sick. An hour after he'd left, she was too weak to move. She asked Ba Leik to buy some electrolyte solutions from the store. The maid brought her some lime juice, which seemed to settle her stomach, but then she vomited. Ba Leik fetched a doctor. He examined her. He said she had a stomach flu, but she should get a check-up at the clinic. Did she want to come now? She shook her head.

He gave her a prescription for some capsules and a syrup, which she gave to Ba Leik who returned in half an hour. After drinking it, she felt bloated and drowsy. She asked Ba Leik to take her to Ma Lin, as she was feeling worse. At Ma Lin's, she called Hkun Pan Sing's wife but she could not come, although they discussed the symptoms on the phone. She said it sounded like a stomach flu or sunstroke. She ought to get some rest and drink lots of fluids. She would do a full check-up tomorrow. Ma Lin promised she would try to get hold of Michael in the meantime. Although Ma Lin asked her to stay at the house, she just wanted to return to the hotel and sleep. But, back at the hotel, she felt even worse than before. The maid and Ba Leik conversed. He told her he could take her to see someone. Too ill to understand, she nodded. He said something else which she did not understand. She got in the car with their help.

✌

When I opened my eyes, the car was past the caves. There was a blur of brightly coloured shirts, sunshades, and cameras, and then it was gone. A few tour buses stood beyond the cluster of tourists. At a bend in the road, the river appeared, thick, grey, unwinding sluggishly like a python after a meal. A village flew by on the left. Then there was a clearing and some fields where ploughs moved against the hills. Women were in the paddy fields bending and holding their lungis up to their knees in the water.

Then we were speeding again past the lake, which opened up on the right. Egrets, snipe, and cranes were in the water. Gulls flew and called raucously. After a while that was gone and we were climbing. The trees were different, the lushness overpowering. The heat built up inside the car. Ba Leik rolled down the window. The rush of air played on my face like a woollen glove.

The car slowed. Several army lorries were parked on the edge of the road. Some soldiers with rifles waved us on. He drove slowly. To the left near a ditch, a group of men in tattered green were kneeling, their hands bound. I thought that they looked like the group from the convoy of lorries that we had seen yesterday. Soldiers stood by with carbines at the ready. A guard who was smoking suddenly flicked away his cigarette, stiffened to attention, and threw a salute. A figure with the unmistakable swagger and authority of an officer was walking past him. He was talking to an aide as he strode towards the group of rebels. Without seeing his face, I was sure that it was Sao On Kya whom I had seen in a colonel's dress. All this unfolded rapidly, in a matter of seconds. Ba Leik glanced at me in the rearview mirror and accelerated. We didn't say anything.

The car plunged down a track into a corniche. The windscreen was full of greenery. Who knew there could be so many shades of green? In my sleep, I felt the car groan and shudder as it climbed up a hill again and went down. The motion made me nauseous, and I felt like telling him to stop but I didn't know how. The car was bumping and pitching and rolling. Finally, we were on a dirt track high up somewhere. We wound past a scree by the hutments. To the left ran a stone wall, made of slate piled like tiles on a roof. The tops of trees in the corniche flashed by like a green fringe topping the wall.

Suddenly, Ba Leik stopped the car at the end of the road. A red hen cackling with alarm ran away. He got out and walked over to the edge. What was he doing? It was puzzling until I realized that he was unbuttoning his trousers. After he had finished, he fished in his breast pocket for a cigarette and matches. Lighting one, he walked towards the car and yanked the door open.

"Here," he said.

I tried to stretch towards the opening but my leg had cramped. Reaching in, he pulled and unglued me from the rexine. The smoke was in my face. My legs were rubbery.

"Come," he said, shading his eyes with his hand as he measured the distance to the path that dipped below the outcrop. He pushed me along the boulders quite roughly with his palm. "Walk. Walk. Go, go."

I nearly fell twice but he didn't stop. I must have climbed for half an hour but he kept urging me on. I saw a thin stream of water trickling over the rocks. A waterfall. Where were we? A muntjac ran out of the woods. I saw the furrows on its forehead. As if it was thinking hard about something. Then it bounded over the tracks into the trees, gone from sight. Ba Leik crooked his arm after it like a gun, pressed an imaginary trigger, and went "dhoom." He laughed.

A water tank loomed up. He pointed to the stairs.

"Go."

"I can't swim."

"No swim. Go. Up. Go."

I climbed, and the smell of algae became stronger. I sensed his gaze on my legs as I walked up.

"Go, go."

I shuddered. I remembered the time we'd sneaked into the colonial club and swum through the water, moving the scum aside. Something stirred. My stomach heaved. Did he mean to drown me?

"No, I can't swim," I repeated. The nausea was stronger. I felt like vomiting. My legs were waterlogged and heavy.

Instead of replying, he pointed.

Then I saw it, the path along the water tank leading into the hillside. He gestured, jump the railing. I did. Then we were on the grass again, walking over the top of the hillock. A corona of mosquitoes had settled on the top of my head. I tried swatting them away. They buzzed and followed.

"Here." He pointed to a defile leading down into a leafy glade. I could smell smoke. I stumbled down, my legs walking on their own, feeling their way. Soon, there was a clearing but the place was empty. His hand was in the small of my back, pushing me along, the other now cradling my elbow. I panicked as he led me to what appeared to be a blank stone wall.

"Where are we? What is this place? Where are you taking me?"

I saw now that he had led me to an entrance in the rockface. Near it lay wooden beams with carvings like those I had seen in the temples. I parted the pieces of sacking that hung from the cave mouth. I felt a push and pitched forward into the cave, barely able to keep my balance.

The lights from the many lamps blinded me. I gagged on entering. There was the sweetness like that of rotting flesh and the smell of sweat. A hand touched my silver bracelet. The touch was rough and scaly like a snake moving on me.

nd was white, scabid-looking, and fingerless. I screamed. Other limbs appeared: some stumps, some forms without noses or ears and eyes. They stood in their dirty lungis, quietly looking at me, all thirty or forty of them.

"The blessed ones," Ba Leik Sin whispered as he bowed, palms together.

I wanted to scream again, but my senses and limbs kept drawing me in against my will. Silently.

We were moving inside another tunnel. This must be vast, I thought.

"Yes it is," came a voice as serene as a lake. "It was part of an underwater-cave system that was found after the river had deserted us over the course of time, just like everyone else. Come." She put her hand on my sleeve. I watched her, unable to move. The skin on her face had thickened all over into white patches. Even that could not mask her efficiency and her air of command. I felt calm as if in the hands of a nurse. My pain was replaced by curiosity. It wound tighter in my chest like a snake. Suddenly, I was crying like a child worn out by hunger, ready for bed.

"It's all right. We've been waiting."

I knew I shouldn't have, but I raised my hand over my mouth and nose to keep out the thick pungent smoke that tickled my nostrils and searched my senses. I sensed Ba Leik at my side.

"Come relax. Don't be afraid, child. I'll take you to her. I'll get my husband first," she said to me, then turned to Ba Leik. "Leave us. You can go now."

AHMAD SAIDULLAH

I didn't see Ba Leik leave. I don't remember how long I sat on the bamboo settee, looking at the people who stared at me silently. The woman returned with an old man with spectacles who sat down opposite me, his hands folded over his belly. His face was gnarled and knobbly, but his eyes were alive with intelligence. His ear was missing. He looked at me long and carefully. Suddenly, I realized he was speaking to me. I strained forward to listen, my back miraculously supple and free of tension.

The curtain lifted, and I caught a glimpse of something gleaming. Then an old woman struggled to walk over, leaning on her good leg. Her skin hung in wrinkles about her like an elephant's. She placed her right stump on my head.

"Be still, my child. Don't be afraid."

The old woman began to speak in a stream of words. They sounded like the ancient texts that Michael would recite.

"She says it's a propitious day. She knew you would come today." His speech was measured and pedantic.

"But how? I just arrived two days ago."

"She is wise. That's why you are here. Today is the celebration. You'll see. I'm Po. Have a pipe."

Someone—I think it was the professor's wife, my nurse—placed before me a long pipe with a bubbling brown ball. Hesitatingly, I raised it to my lips. The thick, pungent draw choked me. Then I tasted its sweetness. I took another puff. It was like inhaling flowers and incense. The nausea fell away and gradually everything became clear. I was distant, I was lifted. The illusions fell away.

The hand was white, scabid-looking, and fingerless. I screamed. Other limbs appeared: some stumps, some forms without noses or ears and eyes. They stood in their dirty lungis, quietly looking at me, all thirty or forty of them.

"The blessed ones," Ba Leik Sin whispered as he bowed, palms together.

I wanted to scream again, but my senses and limbs kept drawing me in against my will. Silently.

We were moving inside another tunnel. This must be vast, I thought.

"Yes it is," came a voice as serene as a lake. "It was part of an underwater-cave system that was found after the river had deserted us over the course of time, just like everyone else. Come." She put her hand on my sleeve. I watched her, unable to move. The skin on her face had thickened all over into white patches. Even that could not mask her efficiency and her air of command. I felt calm as if in the hands of a nurse. My pain was replaced by curiosity. It wound tighter in my chest like a snake. Suddenly, I was crying like a child worn out by hunger, ready for bed.

"It's all right. We've been waiting."

I knew I shouldn't have, but I raised my hand over my mouth and nose to keep out the thick pungent smoke that tickled my nostrils and searched my senses. I sensed Ba Leik at my side.

"Come relax. Don't be afraid, child. I'll take you to her. I'll get my husband first," she said to me, then turned to Ba Leik. "Leave us. You can go now."

I didn't see Ba Leik leave. I don't remember how long I sat on the bamboo settee, looking at the people who stared at me silently. The woman returned with an old man with spectacles who sat down opposite me, his hands folded over his belly. His face was gnarled and knobbly, but his eyes were alive with intelligence. His ear was missing. He looked at me long and carefully. Suddenly, I realized he was speaking to me. I strained forward to listen, my back miraculously supple and free of tension.

The curtain lifted, and I caught a glimpse of something gleaming. Then an old woman struggled to walk over, leaning on her good leg. Her skin hung in wrinkles about her like an elephant's. She placed her right stump on my head.

"Be still, my child. Don't be afraid."

The old woman began to speak in a stream of words. They sounded like the ancient texts that Michael would recite.

"She says it's a propitious day. She knew you would come today." His speech was measured and pedantic.

"But how? I just arrived two days ago."

"She is wise. That's why you are here. Today is the celebration. You'll see. I'm Po. Have a pipe."

Someone—I think it was the professor's wife, my nurse—placed before me a long pipe with a bubbling brown ball. Hesitatingly, I raised it to my lips. The thick, pungent draw choked me. Then I tasted its sweetness. I took another puff. It was like inhaling flowers and incense. The nausea fell away and gradually everything became clear. I was distant, I was lifted. The illusions fell away.

Seated on the bench, I inhaled again. Don't overdo it. Someone came in again, and I saw the dull gleam of that something behind the curtain.

"I was sick at the hotel. The maid told Ba Leik Sin to bring me here. She said the old woman could help," I said, the words coming without bidding.

The man translated this to the crone, who laughed. She said something.

"She'll help. You'll also help us."

"How? I don't understand."

The woman passed her stump over my body. She muttered something.

"My child," the old man translated, "she says you are... big."

"What?"

"Gravid."

"Pregnant," said the nurse.

Pregnant! How could I have been so stupid? All the symptoms but I, Michael—neither of us—could have expected that. Wait, but when? I hadn't...not for a year. My world quivered.

Pammi, I wanted my daughter. Pammi. Where was Pammi?

"No good," he translated. "Don't worry. She'll give you something for it."

I recalled saying, "I have to lie down," as I stretched out on the bench. Another pipe appeared, and I drew in the thick, sweet fumes. I felt as if I was being raised to the skies and the light. Below me was darkness. I looked down at the snakes intertwined, their tails in each other's mouths, fangs ready to pierce. My protectors. I don't know how long I was lost in my thoughts.

The nurse placed a bowl of chased silver brimming with aromatic coals under my nose.

"Breathe," she commanded. I did as she asked. Attar and rose-scented smoke pierced the brain. I woke from my stupor.

Another hand was holding a bowl full of brown liquid.

"Drink this," my nurse ordered.

It had the taste of earth, oils, and herbs. I felt a rush of nausea. I vomited thrice. Each time, a clear spongy ball of phlegm like a frog's spawn came out. God, I'm dying.

Minutes later, a bowl of pineapple appeared.

"Do as my wife says. Eat," he urged, "you must eat."

I was hungry. I shovelled it in. I gagged. The fruit was raw, not ripe. The taste was sour and sharp. The acid cut my tongue.

"Eat," he said again, "now drink this."

I gulped down another bowl. The liquid was viscous and made me sick again.

The others watched.

The old woman was here again. She clapped her fingerless hands. I drained another bowl. I felt light-headed at once, the nausea and backache forgotten. What did it matter if I died now? Images danced in front of me. I was flying like an eagle. I saw a lark above me. I climbed, it swooped, I dived. I saw cities and meadows. The world was full of colours. The yellow was restful, so was the green. The red made me dizzy, but the white, the white erased everything. This sick, beautiful world.

"The end of the world, our world, in a word." The professor's voice. I passed out in a colourless haze.

Somehow I am outside now. I am seated on a log. I'm flanked by the old professor on the left and his wife, the nurse, on the right. I can still see, feel, hear, and think, although the world is growing dimmer. The end seems sharper. The trill of a flute reaches me and then some drums. A middle-aged man advances to the centre of the ground, which serves as a stage and announces the death of the world. Their powers were lost after the curse laid on their ancestors a thousand years ago before the coming of Someone the Golden. After this, there is a musical interlude, loud and discordant. I want the music to be louder, to drown me in it. I make out a boatload of warriors, just landed, who confront another group. The actors are all cave dwellers. It is a dumb show now. There are sword fights. Some are killed or maimed on either side. The king wins the battle and orders a temple to be built.

There is a lull.

"This is Anawrahta the Golden," says the professor in a whisper.

The king wears a costume of shiny gold paper. He orders his soldiers about. He listens to the courtiers and his wives, one of whom wears a sandalwood thanaka on her forehead. The bamboo clapper announces the next scene. A monk arrives and pleads with the king. Anawrahta sheds his cloth of gold to reveal a monk's robe. Workmen rush to build temples. The orchestra erupts in a volley of brass and trills.

He marches to another town. He orders the rival king to surrender his scriptures. He refuses. Anawrahta defeats him in battle and returns bearing an old manuscript. Craftsmen and artisans follow with their wares. He orders more temples to be built.

"The unknown book of the dead. The funerary rites for the end of the world. All part of the pittaka," says the professor's wife. "My husband's studied this."

The king sets out on another march. After this victory, he orders something to be built. His hands shape a stupa. He opens the stupa, removes the relics, and leaves tablets inside.

"After seizing the ports, he became very rich and powerful," the professor says, his eyes gleaming. "Now the interregnum."

The narrator has returned. The professor translates. Do I remember the names accurately?

"Honour to the wise one. 1628 years after the buddha, Sri Tribhuvanadityadhammaraj was crowned king of Arimaddanpur. His beloved wife was Trilokavatamsakadevi."

"This is Kyanzittha's ascension nearly nine hundred years ago. We are all Hulaing Min's descendants in a way, Vaishnavites and Buddhists," his wife adds.

This king is tall and grave. He stands beside an elephant with his five queens, one of whom is the old woman.

The professor says, "Khin Ohn from Pegu, Khin Tan from Htilaing, Abeyadana from Bengal, Thambula of Kyaungbyu, and our queen Uhsaukpan, also called Trilokavatamsakadevi. In reality, Uhsaukpan was Thambula's niece.

"Yes, she is her real descendant, our queen," the professor adds.

Three groups of villagers step forward. The king points them out to his queen. The villagers prostrate themselves in front of the pair.

"What's this?" I whisper to the professor.

"He gives three villages of slaves to his wife—Rapay, Henbuiw, and Sakmunalon—and that ornament."

She wears a head ornament made of three jewelled chaplets. The gems look real. The old queen is given a doll in a blanket.

"Ah, her rajakumar, Prince Jeyakhettara."

She makes comforting noises and rocks the child. Then she sighs and swoons, and attendants stand by her side for a while until they start weeping. A needle of sound like a shehnai pierces the gloom.

The king looks bent and tired. He lies on the cot in the middle and calls several monks, his courtiers, and a young man around him.

"That's Mahathir the sage, that, the monk Muggaliputtasisatther, that one, Son, the other one—no, that one—Sumedha, and then those are Sanghasena, Brahmapal, and Brahmadiv, all great monks," the professor points and whispers.

The orchestra lets out a wail. With great difficulty, the king gestures to the young man, his son, and presents the villagers to him as he had done to his wife. They perform an obeisance. The prince bows. He gestures to the workmen to open the second entrance to the cave. He speaks for the first time.

"I, your slave, order this golden buddha to be made for my lord. I give the three glebes, which my lord gave me, to this buddha."

I can see right inside. It glows in the twilight: a golden buddha lit by hundreds of lamps. The king points to the prince, who pours some water on the ground. The orchestra swells to a climax.

"This was enshrined in this cave temple where it has been to this day, but nobody dares to come here," says my interlocutor.

The rajakumar recites the oath, his face up, palms out:

"Whether it be my son or grandson or any other relative who oppresses these slaves in these villages to whom this buddha belongs, may the offender be prevented from seeing the Arimittiya, lord of men, and cursed be his reign and that of his descendants."

The rajakumar's madness is enacted. He's in love with a girl of twelve over whom he neglects his kingdom. He takes her. Her sickness spreads. The villages are sequestered by his command. The Tartar hordes appear. The narrator asks for the suffering to end.

The queen is by my side. She gives me the manuscript. She opens it and points to a verse. The watchers grow and remonstrate. She waves them away. There are three men near me. One says angrily, "You give back book." The others nod. The professor is firm with them and guides me away. "This will go on till tomorrow. You'll know what to do and when it ends." A lone stringed instrument picks out the epilogue.

The queen and the professor's wife have disappeared into the caves. Ba Leik Sin has appeared out of nowhere to take me back, holding me by the elbow. I watch the professor fade into the shadows. Soon, the evening will fold over the scene like an ink blot covering all traces of light. What does it mean? We are moving up the hill and along the sides of the water tank. I feel dry and hot. The night will drop on us with the suddenness of a stage curtain. The end will come soon, I hope.

I cry out as I stub my foot on the root of a tree. At once, he switches on a torchlight although it is still bright.

"Okay?"

The urgency in his voice is gone, or has it fled from me?

I am skipping over the ground. I barely feel the effort, but he keeps urging me to go faster. I feel an edge of pain. A tall blade of grass has slashed my arm under the elbow. I imagine that it has turned white before it crimsons at the brim. The throb excites me. I look up. The stars have appeared. The night will be painful. There is a moon that's whitening like my scar.

"Madam, quick."

Ba Leik is still leading me by the hand but pauses when I do. I nod and move forward. The trees are bowed, and the sound of a lone crow reaches me. I seem to recognize the wall that we have just passed. Yes, I'm sure of it. But we keep going. How far now? The world is a different place in the shadows, less differentiated, incalculable, anonymous, safer. I don't remember the distances exactly now. This is quicker. Just as suddenly, we are at the car. He opens the door. I subside into the plasticky stickiness. The engine starts at once.

The beams light up two cats. They blink and skitter as the car lurches forward. He begins reversing with a grinding noise.

"Hotel quick, madam," he says as he turns his head to back up the car along the path, his arm along the top edge of the seat. I sense his urgency now. The darkness will enclose us in its fist. Be afraid. The car bowls out to the rutted path where it widens. I pitch forward. We go up and down, the gears whining.

Soon I fall asleep. At times I get up. We are passing the place where I had seen Sao On Kya, I'm sure of it. Under a searchlight, a soldier in a jeep is directing a dumper. It is pouring dirt into the ditch where the prisoners had knelt. I sleep again but I have dreams.

The noises of the town wake me up. We are near the market. The car slows down. They are milling around the car. They are dressed in white, with red headbands. They are carrying lit torches and banners. Some carry staffs and noisemakers and loudspeakers. Others lead the crowd into slogans. They walk towards the police station. I can see a line of soldiers in green. A voice comes over a megaphone, demanding this and that. I open the manuscript, hold it up against the light, and try to read the formula.

As I reach the end, the driver shouts. At the head of the road heading us off are six or seven soldiers, dappled in the car beam. He presses the accelerator as I shout no. I see a figure, head back, winding up to throw something. Another jumps to avoid the impact, and I see a hand bring something down. The car swerves, and there is a thud as something very hard hits us. My world breaks in an explosion of glass.

Suddenly, everything is before me. All the images that had unspooled without sound now deafen me with noise. I faint from the white heat of memory. When I wake up again, we seem to have gone several miles before stopping. I cannot see ahead. Everything in front of me has shattered.

Ba Leik unlocks the door and steps out. He checks the front of the car and returns to fetch a tire iron. He carefully knocks the windscreen, which had shattered into an intricate web of diamonds. The windscreen buckles and then collapses inward. Some shards fall inside. He swears. He ties a towel around his arm, and makes wide sweeping motions on the bonnet and the dashboard, clearing out the crystals. The air plays soothingly warm about my temples. There is that moon. I close my eyes and the images spark to life.

I am carrying a camera. This is near an Uummannaq settlement. A bulldozer is flattening the houses and the area beyond. A loader scoops up the dirt. It throws the earth into different piles. A crane with a Danish company's logo on the side stands idle, ready to begin the construction of the fishing plant. I stand in the middle of some protesters. There is a small clutch of twenty or so activists, workers, and some migrants from Pakistan and Ghana. They are holding up placards: "Leave our burial grounds alone" and "Free our people: empty the jails." Two police officers chat with some troopers in white, from what I presume is an alpine unit, whose car, white with black tracks, is parked by the crane. The protesters blow on whistles, and a voice comes through a megaphone with a staccato. Syllables pour out like hail. Here is the morphology of occupation, of suffering, of a speck in a larger world.

The storm arrives without warning. Suddenly, everything turns white. The sun goes grey. The houses are cancelled by the swirling drifts and fade until they can't be seen. The snow keeps coming as if someone is tipping a cruet. The ice and water on the ground shine like mercury. Wraith-like vapours lift. The machines are still and then elided from sight. Gone, the police, the army, the protesters. The piles of dirt take on the shape of hills in a primordial winterscape. From a distance come the crack of ice and the mournful sound of ships. Then all is muffled.

Near me, I can see the tangles of roots covered in snow reaching into the earth for comfort. The few trees there seem to move in the mist like ghosts, ready to take back what was taken from them. There is menace in the stillness; the beauty is minatory. The few forms I can see are runes, signifying the end. Everything seems remote and pristine. This is a canvas, a white dot on a white world, not a terrain that will hold an encroacher's footprint. It is the erasure of time and history. It is a telluric mystery, the creation of another world, restoring to the dispossessed a primordial vision, a world reclaimed, of whiteness overcome by whiteness. I stop the camera.

⁂

The mist lifts and something stirs again in the sandy pit of my mind. There, I see myself in my flat wearing my apron, stirring something vigorously. The open stockpot bubbles and hisses. I've tried simmering it, taking it out, tenderizing it, hammering away at it but it's still uncooked. I've been trying for three hours. The windows are all open, but the fresh air fails to siphon away the smell from the flat. I've added spices to mask the aroma, but it seems to permeate everything.

There's some furious knocking at the front door. I ignore it until the third bout. I open it to find a pudgy, curly-haired, red-faced man in his mid-twenties, carrying two plastic bags full of papers.

"I just moved in next door. Sorry to ask, but there's this awful pong. What is it?"

"Just some meat," I admit embarrassedly. "Do you know of a quick way to cook whale blubber?"

"Where on earth...whale blubber? Good god, no, I don't, but I could find out, I s'pose."

"Greenland," I say.

"Greenland? Oh, of course, that explains it, ha...oh, this, your computer, is it connected? Can I use it? Close this, what's this, an editing suite?"

"Yeah."

"Okay, here's one. You don't have all this, I imagine. Still worth a try. I'm curious now. Got an apron?"

"Take mine."

We get busy in the kitchen. I tell him about the interviews with native inmates and immigrants at the second-anniversary celebrations of the Erfalasorput and how this woman had given me this piece of whale meat and I had put it in the hotel freezer and sneaked it past customs. He laughs between demands for condiments and spices, and tells me that he is working on his thesis on late religious South Asian epigraphy.

After two hours, we give up. Others have come to complain about the smell. We wrap the hot and dripping pink, white, and grey mess in some issues of *Statstidende* and take it downstairs to the rubbish tip where the cats fight over it.

From his flat, Michael produces a tabbouleh salad, tzatziki, and some retsina quickly, after which he leaves to do some work. I invite him over the next day for an Indian meal. We meet occasionally afterwards and, after sorties in each other's kitchens, sleep together. He brings me back several things from his trips. The last was this silver bracelet from Taxco.

Hold on to this. Don't forget. Recite, remember. Keep it in amber.

I'm with Michael in his parents' house. We had taken the train to Wapping and a taxi to the house. A tall, old man who is having an asthma attack opens the door.

"Ah, Polson. A bad one? Everybody home?" asks Michael, handing him our stuff. Polson holds up my leather jacket with a dubious sniff.

"Yes, Master Michael," he wheezes after a pause.

I tease him lightly as we move down the hall, "And who keeps butlers these days, Master Michael?"

Although the words are deprecating, I sense his pride.

"Ah, Polson. Useless fellow, really. Should have been put out to grass long ago, but grandpa needs him."

His mother, who comes out of the kitchen, coos her confusion. "'Her vowels are as flat as the veldt they came from,'" he says, quoting a writer.

"Glad to meet you. I must say I expected someone quite different. Michael said you came from Greenland," she says.

We go into the drawing room. I see some photographs in heavy silver frames. Michael joins me by the mantelpiece, and we look at each in turn as his mother stands in the doorway.

"Très chic, Michel," I say to him.

"Wants to make an impression. That's her in her Schiaparelli and Mikimoto. You are important. Oh, that's a boating trip. That's Uncle Matt—died two years ago—his wife, Aunt Sally, his daughter and son—they're in Cape Town now. They were in to Canada before, Timmins, I think. Didn't have anyone around for miles. Came back double quick. That's Alex from school who spent the summer with us. Wonder where he is. Africa, I think," he says in a whisper.

"Ah, the snaps," his mother notes, joining us. "That's Green Point. You can't miss Michael. See his scowl? He always has this mane and that bent neck in all of them."

"Mother always called it my 'dying duck look,'" he says with what almost sounds like relish. "That hair. The headmaster didn't like the fashion. He used to keep a pair of scissors in his cassock and round up the boys. At three, he'd troop them into the bicycle shed and shear them off. And that wasn't all. He would then singe the hair. Claimed that was the only way to 'seal the tubes' and stop them rotting. When you came to fetch your bike after school, you smelled burnt flesh."

His accent has turned flat.

I feel that twinge. *How well do I know him? How well can you know anyone?*

His mother continues, "He always did have good taste in women. I mean, now he won't have to look anymore."

If this had continued, I would have curtsied. I swear.

His father is here. He has the clipped look of a military man. He has sparkling eyes and a brush moustache. He wears tweeds. He wipes his hands on them.

"Jeremy. How do? I've turned up at last. Along the edges in this weather. Haven't they offered you a drink yet? Shocking. Won't shake your hand. Been at the pigs. I take it you wouldn't care to see them right now."

"Darling, I've already asked for tea," Michael's mother responds.

"Tea? Deuced hot for that. P–o–l–s–o–n."

His mother winces. The wheezing butler enters and glares at Jeremy.

"What will you have, dear? Ruksana, isn't it? Pretty name. Some amontillado? And you, dear? Your gin fizz? Master Michael will have his malt, I expect. The usual for me. Can you ask cook to see about the food, Polson? Ruksana, we are not formal here. Shown her the place yet, Michael?"

Michael seems resentful over this rush of words. He mutters something about having just arrived. Jeremy says that's wise as it's still too hot, and anyway the copse looks better after sunset. He is off for a wash and can Michael tell Polson to get the colonel ready for dinner?

We've been walking a little in the garden when the second gong goes. His mother had taken him aside when he came, Michael told me then:

"Darling, is this hot enough for your friend? Should I put some wood on?"

"Mother, it's July. There's no need for that."

"Still, I thought..."

"Please, Mother. Rookie's just as English as any of us."

"All right, darling, you know best. I'll get some tea now, shall I?" Michael's mother says, then rises and steps out of the room for a moment.

Jeremy appears in a dark suit and blue tie. Michael whispers, "They do that to all first-timers. Couldn't be sloppier after that, tweed bags and housecoats and kaftans."

"Darling, afraid the soup's off. So she tells me."

"Ah, never cared for cook's consommé. Too much jelly. She doesn't strain it."

"Oh, darling. Maybe I should have asked cook for vindaloo, but you know how I feel about that. Do you think Ruksana will mind sole?"

"Oh, I love sole."

"Mother, do stop fussing. Everything will be fine."

"Don't embarrass everyone, Nattie. This isn't the Cape, you know."

Michael flares up to say something but stops. His mother flushes.

The conversation turns desultorily to the disappearing countryside and the taxes. Someone has advised him to take up sheep farming, Jeremy says.

"Can you imagine, land lice and all that. Fit only for the Kiwis. Give it to them, I say. Wonderful people, mind you. Still better than ostriches. Isn't that what Matt did in Potchefstroom or wherever, Nattie? Imagine an omelette from that, or even a scotch egg. Last you weeks."

There is a commotion outside the room. Jeremy stands up. A tiny old man with a shock of white hair wearing a dinner jacket with a gold watch chain is wheeled in. Polson and a beefy woman in a nurse's uniform lift him into the chair at the head of the table. Jeremy helps.

"Ah, Father," Jeremy says loudly and slowly, "we have a guest."

"Hello, Grandpa. You look wonderful," says Michael.

"Polson," says his grandfather, ignoring the cues and pointing his fork at me, "who's that?"

"Master Michael's friend, sir."

"She won't do. She won't do at all. Take her away, Polson. You know I like them bigger."

I almost get up but sit down after I feel Michael's light, restraining touch on the arm.

"And, Polson, tell that boy Michael not to gulp his food like a dog. Chew, boy, chew, fletcherize. Always had dreadful manners. Pissabed." The spittle dribbles down his chin.

I can feel Michael's anger swell perceptibly. The nurse wipes away the old man's drool with a napkin, but he waves her away.

"Yes, sir. Some sole?"

"Sole, Polson, that's a treat. Filleted, I hope. No bones like last time. She won't get rid of me like that. Ah, we used to go to the creek to fish, the boy and I. Caught some whoppers in our time, eh, Jeremy?"

"Yes, Father. Creek's dry now, though."

"Rivers, lakes, all done. All chaff, all flesh is grass. Even the nice ones. Ibbotson, he was a one, remember? What was that thing that we used to recite on the marches? How did it go, Polson? I know.

'There was a young girl of Aberystwyth
Who took grain to the mill to get grist with
The miller's son, Jack,
Laid her flat on her back
And united the organs they pissed with.'"

"Father." Jeremy puts down his fish fork and pushes his chair back.

The old man starts chortling, a series of drawn-out chuckles that ends in coughs and whistles. He claws at his fly. The nurse slaps his hand.

"And you, madam," says the old man, suddenly tilting his head at Michael's mother, "who let you in? No whores in the mess. No whores! Think I don't know that you want me to choke on the bones? Take your blasted fish back to your hovel. You fishwife. Meretrix, hetaira," he screams and throws the plate at her.

It lands on the wall with a crash. Michael's mother trembles but does not move. She stays bowed over her plate as if she were saying grace again, and cries softly.

The fit passes quickly. The old man has gone quiet and limp like a rag doll. His white head lolls to the side. He begins snoring. Jeremy stands over him. They lift the sleeping figure easily out of his chair, and put him in the wheelchair.

Michael moves across to console his mother.

"Don't mind me, darling. It's just nerves. But what must Ruksana think of us?"

We both make more soothing noises. She nods and tries to compose herself with a deep breath.

When Jeremy returns, the meal continues as if nothing has happened. He talks about his new interest in theosophy and the numen and the Roerich Museum. Michael whispers from time to time to his mother, who is pale and withdrawn. We finish the gooseberry fool with some malvoisie.

"Hmm, films. That's super. Made any that I have seen, Ruksana? No one good here since Carol Reed. There was this American fellow. Welles, very clever. Now this Greenway lad, he's promising," Jeremy says.

"I'm afraid I just make documentaries."

"Ah, so you don't get the paparazzi tailing after you," says his mother, a little recovered.

"Grandpaparazzi, more like," Michael says. "Her last on the Greenlanders also got its share of grandmamarazzi."

"Ooh, Michael, you are far too naughty to say such things." The colour is back in her cheeks but she looks shaky. "I have a head. Excuse me, Ruksana. I am sorry but I must go. It gets so difficult at times."

After a walk through the garden and a nightcap, Jeremy drives us to the station.

"He's much worse, Dad," Michael says.

"Yes, needs a nurse round the clock now. Hates doctors. Polson can't manage," his father responds.

"Yes, time Polson retired. It's a strain on Mother to look after two invalids."

"She's been getting these headaches, migraines, but he won't. Too devoted. His daughter was here from Bristol. He wouldn't go. 'I serve the colonel' and all that rot. Matron's okay but a bit too rough. Anyway, here's Shadwell."

You've made a lot of progress.

How much more enjoyable it had been when I had stayed by myself in that flat in Malá Strana before he came. I had been in the tenements to talk to the Roma families, the bright-eyed children, the adults, suspicious and wheedling in turn. I had gone to the hernas where I found the men who had run away from Jeseník after their houses had been attacked and firebombed. Some had been beaten. Two were killed. Those who had resisted had been arrested. Police and racist thugs were behind it, they said. Anyway, the jails are full of us. Some have died by their own hands there; others in mysterious circumstances. Our women have been sterilized by force as undesirables, some policy.

Here, we cannot afford the stoves and furniture and have to live in close quarters. Evictions are common. They won't allow our children to attend the normal schools. Landlords are throwing us out of Žižkov. Most are moving to Plženská or Karlín. Nobody will give us jobs. In turn, I tell them ironically about how a bouncer refused me entry to an Indian eatery on Dlouha. We laugh, although I sense some resentment which is not spoken.

After he arrived, we walked hand in hand to the pink tank and walked on the embankment under the metal bridge that led to Letná and where that statue of Stalin had once stood. Michael approached the man in the black peacoat in the nearest boat.

"We just have forty-minute cruises. The locks have been raised. We have a recorded tour in English. Next one leaves in an hour."

Michael paid the man after asking the price. He was furious.

"Where's the rest of the money? We gave you a hundred."

The man pointed to me and went off with a hurt look.

"He gave it to me. Here."

"I guess we should come back in half an hour."

We walked, studying the clouds and watching the crowds move along the Karlův Most.

"Fuck, it's too cold. Let's go in and get a drink."

In the cabin, they had set up a bar. A Russian woman was laying in boxes of soft drinks.

"I'll try a hot grog. What about you?"

"No, just a coffee."

The woman brought the drinks. He tore two sachets of sugar precisely along the dotted lines, and added them to the grog.

"God, this stuff is strong. Really warms you up. Try?"

I took a sip and gagged at the fumes.

"Still, you've got to admit it's better than the gluggwein in Brno."

"I'll stick to hot chocolate next time."

"Shall we go upstairs now? I see some people. We should get a seat. Wait, another grog."

The woman collected his fresh cup, my coffee, and put them on a tray and went up.

I walked behind Michael and noticed how he had wobbled. Sharp woman.

The benches were hard and the wind made us shiver. He moved across me so I wrapped myself in the blanket.

The tape started up with a crackle. The sound turned muddy in the breeze, the words indistinct. I'd seen everything before so I looked at him. He snapped a couple of photographs, the flashes blinding me.

"Stop that," I said.

His face was flush with grog. His eyes swivelled.

"What's he saying? I can't hear anything," he asked with a slur.

"It's about the park."

"Not much to see from down here. Bad idea, this." He stowed his camera in his bag.

The tin voice droned on about the ministry buildings. By the time we neared the bridge, the sun was setting. I saw the roof of the national theatre turn red in the light.

Something had gone wrong with the tape. When we passed under the bridge, the voice instructed us to look at the ministry building on the left bank. A buzz of discontent broke out among the passengers, who looked glazed. I noticed that nobody turned to look at the sights. Everyone was huddled against the cold. Michael had begun to snore. I threw the blanket over him.

I want you to gaze down. Why do you still pull back from the brink?

In the apartment, we laugh at the reruns of German Christmas shows on TV with their sentimentality and lederhosen. We cook and go for walks and runs. Maybe these are not important. Now I am with him on the shores of the river, outside the city. There is a crowd in white. It's a bridal party out near the river for photographs. A man pitches a large fruit into the waves; his dog wades in and retrieves it. I see fisherfolk at sea and hear their cries. A sun and moon are up side by side. I swear I saw them.

I am filming the eagle near the rocky shore. He is reading Hopkins aloud, something about a lark. Suddenly, I slip and fall over. I am swooping like the eagle, down, down, onto the rock. I hear the thud distantly, as if unrelated, and my spine shrieks. I see the blood spreading on my white dress, but I hear his voice continuing to read just before I roll into the water that had looked blue but is green from below. I'm still awake. Everything is taking hours. Throwing the book aside in a run, he jumps in and picks me up like a courtier bearing a gift. He carries me as far as he can, howling aloud before the guests start running towards us and everything turns to a blaze of white.

The ambulance arrives and then it's a blank. How did I get to Motol? Did he tell me about the golf course, the crematorium, on the way? I don't remember any of it. There are months of being hooked to the monitor, that I know. There is the chatter of mothers telling their children "Nech toho, nebo ti jednu fláknu," harried nurses exclaiming "do prdele" as they fumble with equipment, snatches of "cože?" "jako," "počkej," although I'm told I couldn't have seen or remembered any of this. I can't see the gurneys or the surgeons with scalpels and the nurses like Jain nuns with cloths across their noses and Michael there, always there, in that corner with his books and notes, but I know all this is true. The silence is punctuated by the drips and hums of machines. The room is sterile.

How do I remember that night? How do I know, I, who had not even begun, had not been born yet, never born, never alive, never living, and hope never to be, but who feel the violence etched on every synaptic trace? When nobody was looking, how did I see his furtive look round the corridor, feel his weight on my body pressing down, the painful parting of legs, the anxious thrusting, the careful wiping, but not careful enough? He had opened the window afterwards. When I came out of the coma, I smelled the fried potato cake. The bramborák was my first smell. Later, I remembered many sessions with psychologists, men and women in white clothes in white rooms, the colour of sickness.

∽

We reached Htin Aung Kyi's house at ten. Ma Lin rushed to the car. She hugged me and asked Ba Leik what had happened. They examined the car and the windshield. Michael was waiting. He walked over with some exasperation, his tongue darting in and out like a lizard's.

"Rookie, what on earth? Are you all right? I was so worried. Where were you? Did you have an accident? We've been looking since the morning. Things have been crazy here. Sao On Kya and Aung Kyi have got a search party out."

"I'll call him and let them know you are safe," Ma Lin said.

"I wasn't well. Ba Leik took me to see a woman," I explained.

"What woman? Couldn't you have left word?" Michael asked.

"Look, I'm fine. I'm much better." I withdrew from his embrace and touch.

His hands fell to his sides.

Ma Lin watched us with an expression that was hard to read.

I refused the food and drinks that Ma Lin laid out.

"Sorry, Ma Lin, I'm very tired. I want to go to the hotel. Michael, can we? Ma Lin, is it okay if I give Ba Leik some money? He's been with me all day."

I was quiet on the drive back, and pulled back again when he tried to hug me.

At the hotel, he announced it solemnly. I could see he'd been waiting to say it. He was enjoying himself.

"I couldn't tell you this in the car, but Hkun Pan Sing and Ezekiel and Pilar were arrested this morning. Caught trying to bribe officials into smuggling out rubies, Htin Aung Kyi said. Sao On Kya found out."

I thought with shock of Pilar in a prisoner's garb, this woman barely out of her bridal gown who wanted to build houses, caught in flight like a bird, a poor white pigeon with her two fledglings.

"The doctor was very upset too. She was at Htin Aung Kyi's. She blamed me for introducing the Jacobs. He did too. I can't imagine why. I didn't. They must have met later."

I didn't say anything about Sao On Kya.

Then he turned all solicitous. He unpacked some biryani and kawabs with a flourish.

"Look, I bought these for you. Eat something. I bet you haven't eaten anything all day, have you?" he asked.

When I retreated from these questions, he asked another.

"What's wrong? You've changed somehow. You all right?"

I pretended I was too tired to talk and fell into bed. I wedged a pillow between us and kept awake the entire night, mindful of his closeness.

The southern temples stood like giant beehives. We skirted the ones we had already seen. He admired the woodcarvings. He was at my side when I produced the manuscript and started reading from it. He looked curiously at the text, but did not move to take it from me. I was aware of him. I saw him as an alien, a figure of hormones, lymph, and plasma, a ship without moorings, and I was flooded with doubts. *Who am I? Who is he? A conglomerate of discrete events? A mass of responses as conditioned as rats in a lab? An agent? A receptacle? Whose land am I? Who tills me, fills me, and takes me over? Is your pain, your story, more important than mine? Who decides? Is pain the only reality and suffering the true one? If you erase me, do I matter, do I leave a trace? If you cut me, do I not bleed? Does it matter if I am alive, will it matter when I am not?...*

It was as if I had returned to dip in the swimming hole where I used to bathe only to find that the current had changed. I remembered his banal remark. "I am so depressed when I return from one of my trips to find that the world had gone on so well without me." Then I thought of his kindness to my child, of his way with boys and girls, but I was resolved. It was time.

I began to recite the formula slowly, taking care over the words that rolled sonorously over my tongue, rushing to get out after the gaps of centuries, to be let loose on the world like furies. At the end, I took a lighter as he watched horrified and confused. I lit the pages and watched the smoke wisp, the tail of letters lapping the heart of the secret with a red tongue. I saw the fresco of the tanaka on the left develop a seam and crack like a whip. I heard the tearing somewhere deep in the bowels under my feet, and felt the landscape dissolve in a gaudy vision of demons, buddhas, lotuses, and beasts.

"Run, Rookie, run," he shouted, trying to drag me, but I resisted. "Earthquake."

The brickwork, posts, lintels, the buddha wavering and toppling, shuddered and cracked and came cascading. A fragment of a cornice hit me on the temple and I swayed as I was dragged into the gaping wound, and through the opening of the temple door I saw the nat tumble and the spectres of dust rise like dervishes on the shaking plain as far as I could see before the central post fell and the ceiling came closer, closer, and I raised my arms with a glimpse of the snakes as the world closed over us in a shroud of whiteness.

THE BLINDING DARKNESS

He came when the rivers had dried. The animals lay dying and birds fell from the skies. The earth resembled a crazy map of cracks and lozenges. Old people sat on their cots under the dead trees, and looked at the stubble wilting in the sun and the skeletons of fish that lay baked on the riverbed. Devils of dust blew up from the arid ground. Dust coated the faces of those who sat outside. Dust entered their eyes, noses, and mouths, and reminded them of the death that was waiting for them.

The stranger approached them on foot. He wheeled his bicycle beside him.

"Good people," he said, "why are you all so sad?"

His calm, gentle voice soothed them.

"We had everything," said an elder, swallowing with difficulty. "Now there's nothing. Nothing grows." He gestured towards the fields that lay fallow and the cows that lay almost dead near their posts under the withered trees.

"Many have died. The few children who are left eat dirt."

"We used to find beetles and roots before. Yesterday the children caught a toad and ate it. They eat dirt mostly but the ground is hard. Now we are waiting to die."

"Our young boys and girls ran away."

The stranger reached into a pannier. He brought out a flute and played an air. Suddenly, the trees were green to them, and the sky, a white-hot shroud, turned blue. The blasts of hot wind felt cool on their faces. They thought they heard the sound of birds again.

Their despair stopped, but tears rolled down the face of the elder who had spoken first.

Another old man shook a child who lay sleeping and said, "Take him to the hut. Get him some tea with whatever water she has."

The boy, who had pale skin and pink eyes, looked at the stranger. His eyes teared, and he shaded them from the sun with his hand.

"Go on, go on. What's wrong with you?" the old man urged.

The boy got up hesitatingly. He put on his slippers. He walked ahead, turning his head, and then, as if afraid, took shorter, quicker steps that led to the hut under the acacia tree.

The boy stood at the entrance of the hut and pointed inside. From the hut came a regular clacking noise.

The stranger entered. He peered inside. The place was dark. He could see only the coals and the hissing steam curling in the corner.

A soft hand clutched his. A young girl had come to the door and guided him inside.

The clacking noise stopped.

"Haan, who is it? Speak louder. My hearing's not good, you know," came a cracked voice. She asked again. "Come here, child, let me see. Bring him here."

He was standing by the loom but could not see the old woman who had spoken. Two hands came out of the dark and roamed over his face. They stopped suddenly.

"What do you want?" The voice was harsher and demanding now.

"They told me to come here. Mother, what do you weave in the dark?"

"Where do you come from?"

He pointed towards the entrance.

The girl whispered to the old woman.

"What do I weave? See for yourself."

The girl held his finger and traced it over the patterns like a boy reading a book in school.

"What do you see?" the crone asked.

"That's a hill, a river, isn't it? A cow is tied here. This is an acacia tree like the one outside. Are these trees? There's a man holding something, someone? There are some men and women lying on the ground. Is that a group?"

"Go on."

"They are running after the man."

"Yes, it's not finished but you of all people would not be interested. Girl, give him some tea and weight the shuttle."

Her voice crackled with rage.

He took the clay cup with thanks and squatted outside.

He sipped the brackish tea. He asked the girl how the old woman could weave, being blind and working in the darkness.

"She says that she gets headaches. The world freezes into pictures, she says."

"Is she your grandmother?"

The girl shook her head.

"She is Ganga, my grandfather's eldest sister."

He did not ask any more questions.

The girl skipped to the cot where the boy lay under the tree. Brother and sister talked in whispers.

He went inside and the loom fell silent again.

"What do you want? Why did you come? When do you leave?" the old woman asked.

"Mother, just to return the cup," he said gently. "Mother, why are you so angry?"

She was silent.

"I don't mean any harm. Answer me this, Mother. Why do you weave these painful scenes?"

"They speak the truth."

"Whom does that comfort? Isn't it better to ease their suffering? To make something happier, something that gives pride to everyone?"

"What would you know about that?"

"At least sell your tapestries. With that, you could buy food and grain for everyone. The others have nothing."

"We are paying for what we have done."

"May the mercy of god soften your soul, Mother. You need it like the parched land here needs the rain."

He pulled out his flute and began to play, but the noise from the loom that had started up overpowered his melody.

He went outside and sat with the elders. Their litany began.

"We are dying. We want to be at peace."

"Our children cry. The women have no milk."

"Old people do not rise from their beds."

"The graves are full of weaklings and newborns."

"Our young people ran away. We can only hope they survived."

"We can't even burn the bodies. The river's dried up."

"We used to find fish in the dried riverbed. That kept us going."

"The authorities sent a tanker of water once, but then they wanted money. They know about us."

"They don't help any of the tribals here."

He asked, "Who has robbed you of this? Who stole your crops, you who are the children of the kings of Kausambi? You used to have palaces of marble, and now even your huts are turning to dust in this drought."

They said they did not know. Things just happened.

The stranger picked up his flute and pointed at the other village far away.

"What about the other village? I passed through it. They have everything. Water, food, riches, comforts, happiness."

"They are our brothers although they are different. They have helped us although they didn't have to."

"How have they helped you if you are dying of hunger and thirst?" the stranger asked.

"We sold most of our cattle to them. They paid us well."

"Now your money is gone. You don't have any milk. And you can't feed the cows and goats that are left. Everybody starves."

"It's god's will."

"Can you write something about our plight? Maybe people will read it and come to help us. I can't believe everybody's forgotten us."

"Don't you remember they came to take photographs of us? They gave us some money but they never came back. They didn't send anybody to help us."

"I'll do what I can," the stranger said.

The stranger moved to go but they asked him to stay. He retreated to the posts where the cows lay, their sides heaving. He played his flute, a slow resigned air, which put forgetfulness into the hearts of the old men.

After a while, he stopped playing but stayed squatting and watching them, the flute in his hands.

Nothing moved.

After a while, without anyone noticing it, he left.

The children went into the hut.

"Ganga," said the girl. "I'm thirsty. Tell me a story."

"When I was young," said the old woman as if in a dream, "my breasts were full of milk. I raised many children, not just my own. Oh, I had many. Many that were mine, and others who came to me. They were all mine. But listen to this story."

They listened to the loom in the dark. It spoke to them of harvests, of the song of birds, and the rangoli patterns, which once decorated their thresholds.

"This music makes us sad. The other music makes us forget our hunger and thirst and pains," the boy said.

"Yes," said the old woman quietly. "But this makes you see. How can I tell you that the loom speaks to me? It speaks to you, too. I can't read or write. When it's silent, the cracks in the walls, in the earth, teach me the words."

"What is the use of this?" asked the girl.

The old woman was silent and set to work again.

This time, the loom spelled out a dirge, full of crests of mourning decked in white. It lamented everything that the old woman could not see. It grieved for the fly caught in the spider's web, for the frog in the serpent's throat, for the stork's desperate tries to extricate its leg from the jaws of a crocodile on the banks.

The children fell asleep. They had many dreams.

When they woke up, the old woman was seated beside them. She stroked their foreheads.

"What did you dream?" she asked.

"I had two dreams," began the boy. "I was in a catboat, but it was not on the water. It was sailing on the sand in the desert. Suddenly, there were thunderclouds. It started raining, pouring. Although just before the storm, I had been hot and thirsty and longed for water, now I was afraid of this downpour. It was like a curtain of water that fell. I could not see through the waterfall, and I could no longer control the boat. It lurched and bobbed. Soon, the sand turned to water and everywhere there were huge waves and the boat capsized and I woke up just before I drowned.

"In my second dream, I saw my mother on a cot. She was dying. I knew that because all the people who were near her were crying. The priest was there reciting something. She was trying to tell me something. She stroked my head and clutched me to her breast. But when she put her mouth to my ear, she died. A rat jumped out from between her teeth and nibbled at me. A man took me by the hand and I woke up."

Then the girl spoke.

"I had two dreams as well. In the first, I dreamt that there were many guests at a wedding. There was music and dancing. Everybody was eating and drinking. Suddenly, one man ran between us and smashed our plates and cups on the ground. Then he drew a sword and plunged it into the clay pots, which held the food, yogurt, and the drinks. They shattered. Streams of blood ran out from every one of them.

"In my second dream, I dreamt of a chest in which there were many jewels. There were rubies like pigeons' eyes, diamonds that shone brighter than the snows on the mountains, gold that shimmered like the summer sun, emeralds as large as green mangoes, and sapphires that seemed to be made out of the sky itself, so blue they were. I did not know whose jewels they were but I was tempted to pick them up. I picked up a sapphire but it burned my fingers. It was so hot that I cried out and dropped it. When it hit the floor, the sapphire cracked with the sound of a baby's crying. In every shattered piece of crystal, I saw my face staring back at me but I could not recognize myself. It looked like someone else's face."

The old woman was about to interpret these dreams as she did every morning, when she heard some shouts. The children raced outside.

"It's raining, it's raining, it's raining," shouted the boy laughingly. "Ganga, it's raining."

"There's so much water. The heavens are crying for us, they've taken pity on us," said the girl as she ran to collect all the pots and pitchers she could find. Everybody ran outside. Ganga stayed in her hut.

The old men on their cots gazed up. Their tears mingled with the rainwater and ran down their faces.

"Our rivers will fill up. Soon there will be fish, crops, and fruit."

"Our cows will become fat, and there will be milk and butter, ghee and yogurt."

"Grain will be plentiful. There won't be any shortage of bread or cakes."

"We're blessed."

Within days, the river was full and the brooks began trickling again. Animals that had languished under the trees got up shakily to graze on the shoots of grass that had appeared. Leaves sprouted on trees, and shaded the old men who sat on their cots and wondered.

"When will he come again? Our darkness has lifted."

"This is all the kindness of that stranger."

The few children of the village danced in the showers and played all kinds of games outside, including hop, skip, and jump. They wheeled bicycle rims. Kites rose again into the sky like gaily coloured birds. Families began to sleep outside at night under the light of the moon.

Slowly, the village returned to its old rhythms. Cicadas hummed, birds called, and frogs croaked up to the moon. The sound of laughter returned to the village.

Only the old woman in her hut did not take any joy in the changes or participate in the festivities of thanksgiving. In the hut, the loom wove its implacable narrative.

"Ganga," said an elder who had recovered enough strength in his legs to walk to the hut one day, "are you not glad that our village has recovered and that people are happy now?"

The old woman did not answer. Another elder, who had also come with him, spoke.

"Ganga, you sit in the darkness and believe that the world is full of the blackness that lives in your eyes and heart. What does it take to please you, to make you happy?"

"Imagine when we have enough, you can have the operation on your eye. Soon you will be able to see. You will rejoice when you see the happiness around you once these white webs are removed from your eyes. You always said you felt like someone had spilled some whey into your eyes while you slept."

She did not reply.

Curious at her silence, the elder asked to see what Ganga had woven recently.

The old man rubbed his horny fingers on a tapestry. In the plains warmed by the sun and cooled by the snows in the mountains, he learned that there were two villages not very far from each other. In the spring when the flowers poked their heads through, the people from the village which had oranges, basil, and cows would go over to visit their neighbours who would offer them rose syrup, sweets with nuts and silver foil, and all kinds of rice with raisins, and cheese made from goat's milk.

At the end of summer, the process would be reversed. Now the second village would be fed on the mangoes that had hung, golden and juicy pendants, on the trees, and offered faalsas and jaamuns that revealed their flavours in clay jars. Musicians would play and children would run around the trees, and then the sky looked bluer than before and the air was sweet with the song of birds and the smell of flowers.

Other tapestries spoke of times when the villages worked together. One helped build a dam for a neighbour. The other built a brick kiln in return for the kindness. One sent water and the other helped to build houses. All this went over for hundreds of years, the weaving said. These villages were so well known that they thought of each other as sister and brother. On a certain day, villagers from both sides would meet on the border and tie shiny threads around each other's wrists to prove their family bonds.

Sometimes, there were disagreements. A neighbour's cow would occasionally stray into a field and eat up the roses or scare the goats, but, after a word or two, the cow was restored to the owner and harmony reigned again. Sometimes, a child from the other village chased or teased animals, and words would become as hot as the loo that blew through the plains in the summer. But a word from the women and the children brought peace to the villages.

"I don't understand, Ganga. Why do you dwell on the bad things that happened in the past? Why do you live in that country? We wish you could open your eyes and see what is happening now, and accept the present and rejoice in it."

She spoke finally. Her voice was calm.

"I am blind but will you blind yourself to the truth, you have seen so many events with your own eyes? Listen to this..."

The loom spelled out a tale where one of the villages took the other's women by force. In turn, it said, they burned our place of worship. We killed their cattle. Many died. Our youngsters fled. We violated our pact. We dishonoured our neighbours.

"Ganga, I don't see why you fill our lives with pain and guilt at a time of happiness. We are going."

"These histories that you continue to weave brought us bad luck, I think."

A few days later, the boy came running to the elders under the flowering mango tree.

"It's him. He's here. He's coming. And he's brought them with him as he promised."

He pointed in the direction of the river.

As if by magic, the stranger had appeared. Behind him were some people.

"Respected sirs, I have brought what belongs to you and which was taken from you so unjustly," the stranger announced.

The news spread quickly through the village. Women left off pounding the grain and rushed to the spot.

"Oh, it's my Shankar. He's grown so big."

"Kusum, you're a woman now. Come to my arms."

Soon, the place was full of embraces and joyous laughter for the long-lost children. The elders wiped away their tears.

"How can we ever thank you? You've brought prosperity to our village and happiness to our people."

"I'll do the best I can to help your village. I have my book to guide me."

He smiled when they asked him his name.

"Names don't matter. It was so hot here when I first came. Call me 'Thandai.' Call me anything. I'll rest in the shade in my usual spot."

He sat under the tree and brought out his flute. The boy stood next to him and looked at him through his tearing pink eyes. The man reached out and ruffled his hair. The boy smiled.

"How is Ganga?" he asked the boy.

The boy gestured that she was the same.

"Go and play with your sister. Come to me later. We'll go for a walk. I'll teach you many things."

Ganga asked the children about the stranger.

They debated what he looked like. The boy said he looked like a white man. He wore a suit and smoked a pipe. The girl laughed and said that he wore a dhoti and spoke like any villager. The boy said that one of the elders had said he wore the brahmin's thread; another had claimed that he was circumcised. The old woman trembled and kept quiet.

After a while, she asked the children if they knew where he came from. The boy said that one elder had seen him come down from the hills. Another said he had walked on the riverbed to the village. Others said they had seen him come from a silver airplane. When the elders had asked him where he had come from, he had pointed to the direction of the setting sun.

The old woman fell quiet.

The stranger spoke to the elders.

"You, who are the sons and daughters of kings, need something to remind you of who you are. You, who have suffered so much, deserve something much better, something that is in keeping with your heritage, something to remind you of your days of glory."

"Thandai," one said, "the only reminders we get now are from Ganga. And those mementoes make us feel heavy and sad and worthless."

"Ah," he said gently, "she is an old woman who suffers from the lack of sight. I'll also try to help her. I'll pay for everything."

The elders murmured among themselves and spoke.

"It is up to Ganga to accept the gift of sight that he has offered to her."

"Son, you have been a godsend in good times and in bad times. Our people have been as happy as they can ever remember, even more. We do not have anything to give you to show our gratitude."

The stranger answered with humility.

"I do not help you for any other reason except to help you become what you were once, maybe even greater. Grant me one wish, though. I have one request. It's a simple one. Can you give me this poor orphaned boy so I can look after him like a father and mother?"

The elders conferred and agreed.

"We have decided. You may have the boy if you agree to treat him as your own son and if he does not object. Do you object?" they asked the boy.

The boy shook his head. He said that he was happy with

the arrangement. The stranger hugged him and took him by the hand.

In the evening, the stranger played the flute. Those who heard it felt their chests swell with pride before they fell asleep.

The next day, the stranger went to the hut.

"Mother, where are you?"

"Oh, it's you. What do you want?"

"I want to help, Mother. I hear you need an operation. I can arrange that."

The woman did not say anything.

"I can also help you sell your tapestries in town."

"Oh, I see. What will you take?"

"Not much," he said, after a laugh.

"I am sure."

The following week, the stranger assembled the youth he had brought with him and talked to them for a long time. They listened, rapt, to his words. Most of them nodded when he pointed to a spot.

"Sirs," he announced to the elders, "we will build the palace behind that hut. The book says that there is where the old palace stood."

"A palace? Why do we need a palace now? Anyway, where will you get the materials to build it? We don't have stone or anything. Just wood, wattles, and mud."

"I have asked the young people to look for them. It will be so glorious that nobody will ever forget you again."

"What will you build it out of, Thandai?"

"Something that shines with your glory. Marble, maybe."

"Marble? We don't have marble but maybe the other village…"

The old woman sat at the loom. She had had one of her blinding headaches that morning. The girl sat by her side.

"What will you make today?"

"Your dreams and your brother's. It may be the last I do before the doctor operates on my eyes."

"When will that be?"

"Next week."

"That's when they're going to the other village to ask for the marble."

"When?"

"For the harvest festival. Everybody's been invited. After our harvest, everyone will go over to the village to help them with theirs. It's just like the old stories you tell us, Ganga."

"I won't be able to go."

"Oh, but Ganga, think of it. Soon you'll be able to see how well the cows are filling out. You'll see how happy my brother has become. His eyes, which are always full of tears, now weep with joy. He has new clothes and toys. You will see for yourself how big and strong Shankar Palwalkar has become and how fat Kusum's baby is. She tries to eat everything, even Thandai's book. May everyone be safe from the evil eye."

"Do not take that man's name in this house," the old woman told the girl angrily.

The next day, the work began behind the hut. They started digging the foundations. The old woman heard the shouted commands and the songs of the working men and women in the trench. She heard boys and girls and old men and women joining in the labours.

She spoke to the girl. "Where's your brother? He doesn't come here."

"He's working on the building. He wants me to work too."

"You stay here with me."

"He doesn't allow any machines. He says we have to work with our hands. Machines are not good."

"He does, does he? I thought he uses a bicycle."

The stranger watched the work from under the tree. If the labourers got tired or paused for a break or a smoke, his flute would revive them. Whenever she caught the thin melodies, Ganga would start up the loom, but she could always hear the labourers resume their work with renewed vigour.

One evening, the stranger went to the elders.

"Sirs, the work has advanced. But, for such a grand building, you need to make a sacrifice. For your good fortune, you should offer something precious to the gods."

"Precious? What do you mean by that? We are simple people. We don't have much. We can give food and milk, maybe some money now, a little gold. We have saved a bit, but we also need to keep something for the future."

"Oh, that won't be enough," said the stranger with an understanding smile. "But, don't worry if you don't have anything, I'll give up what's truly precious to me."

The elders looked at each other and smiled. They liked the openness and generosity of this stranger.

Her day arrived.

Shankar and the others carried Ganga on a litter to a makeshift theatre that they had constructed out of canvas and bamboo. After the doctor had examined her, they laid her down on the table.

The stranger stood by her side and held her hand.

"I'll give you something, Mother," the doctor explained, "to help you sleep through the operation. You won't feel a thing. Usually, we do one eye at a time but, in your case, we'll do both. Your children can help you while your eyes are bandaged. Once we take them off, you'll be able to see everything as you saw it in childhood, everything as if you'd never been blind."

One of the nurses spoke gently to her.

"Don't be afraid. No eye strain, remember, Mother. Please don't do any lifting or weaving. You'll have to rest your eyes. Ask the young people here to help you. There are so many. After a few days, we'll check to see if your eyes are well enough so that you can return to your tasks. Do you understand?"

She nodded.

Everybody else, including the stranger, left. The nurses helped the doctor. The routine went smoothly.

When the drug wore off, Ganga awoke to the same darkness. Her eyes were bandaged. Instead of the blinding pain, she felt a burning in the centre of her eyes. She wanted to take the bandage off, but the child held her hand. She gave the old woman some medicine to stop the pain. She went to sleep again.

On the day of the harvest, the fields were full of singing workers. They culled the ears of wheat, which were heavy with grain, and cropped the yellow-headed mustard plants. Youngsters helped to load the corn on to carts. The women spent the afternoon tearing off the husks and silk so that they could make a present of cornmeal to their neighbours.

In the afternoon, the threshing began. Singing, groups of women took turns with the flails, which they brought down on the cut wheat. Sometimes, they paused to gather the separated grain and winnow it. The air was full of husk, which made the animals sneeze.

In the evening, they were all ready, even the old people, with their gifts and harvest implements. Only Ganga and the girl stayed at home. Ganga heard a strange air from the flute for the first time, as if from a distance, which made the blood in her veins course faster. Her heart pounded. She felt the girl's hand flutter in her grip but she held her tight.

"No matter what happens today, stay with me. I am frightened."

The music was fainter, but the old woman was roused.

"Come," she said to the girl, "come. Let us follow. You'll be my eyes."

The pair set out. Although the group had disappeared from sight, they could catch a few strains of the melody that floated in the air.

She clasped her hands over the girl's right ear.

"Don't listen to it, no matter what. Put your fingers in your ears."

They walked slowly until they reached the path that led to the village. Ganga told the girl to stay out of sight.

When the girl led her to the back of the cordoned-off area where the festivities were being held, the old woman asked her to stay quiet and not to move. Again, she admonished the child not to listen to anything.

The girl watched the dumb show. The two groups had met with obvious goodwill. Food and drinks were being shared. Elders from both villages had gathered in another area to confer. They were negotiating something. Sometimes, it looked as if they had raised their voices; at others, they nodded in agreement. But she could not hear what they were saying. She saw the stranger sit apart and follow the discussion without speaking.

Occasionally, the girl would tell the old woman what was happening but, with her fingers in her ears, she could not hear the sound of her own voice or be sure if she had used the right word. From time to time, the old woman would nod.

After a while, it seemed clear to the girl that the elders could not agree, although the others were enjoying themselves with the food and music and dancing.

The girl saw the stranger take his flute out and begin to play. As soon as the old woman heard the notes, she pulled her hands away and put her fingers in her ears.

"Put your hands over your ears. Cover them."

But the girl's arms had grown tired. When she tried to raise them again, they ached. She dropped them to her sides and listened. Although the old woman kept nudging her with her hip, she did not want to leave. The tune began gently. She thought she saw the stars and the sky change colour. Then there was a groundswell like the earthquake that had shaken the rope bridge over the river in Rishikesh, which she had crossed with her family. The tempo quickened. There was a cascade of harsh, discordant notes. These faded. Now she thought she heard drums, which took on the high-stepping lilt of a march. She almost ran into the middle of the gathering, but some force kept her clinging to the old woman's dress somehow.

"What is happening?" the old woman asked the girl. "Speak louder, child. I can't hear you."

She tried to reply but she found that she could not. She burst into tears.

"Let's go," said the old woman, pulling her gently.

As they walked away, she heard the music change. Soon, it had taken on the clashing of swords and the sound of guns being fired and the cries of the wounded. It exhorted; it goaded; it mocked the fear that they felt in their hearts. A flood of red darkened the senses of the revellers. Even the girl, young as she was, felt brave and strong as a lion. Somehow, the closeness of the old woman gave her the strength to fight the urge to run back and join them. She imagined she could see her brother looking through his wet, pink eyes at the flute player who stood by his side. She imagined that, like him, she could die for this man.

Then things began to happen which she could not relate to the old woman. Over the others, there came a darkness that eclipsed all their senses. In their confusion, families called out to each other and groped with outstretched hands. The food and drinks and the harvest grain fell from their hands and spilled on the ground. They felt others grabbing at them and thought they were being attacked. They started to hit out with whatever they could find. Fumblingly, they tore their neighbours' finery, ripped off their jewellery, and gouged their eyes. They swung their weapons. Some fought with their bare hands. The music had stopped.

The girl turned to the old woman who somehow sensed her urgency.

"What's happening? Why don't you tell me what's happening?"

The girl tried to speak again, but she knew that she had lost her power of speech forever. Feeling the tears warm on her hand, the old woman stopped and caressed the child gently. They walked home slowly through the bushes and forest, taking care not to be seen.

When they reached the village, she could hear the shouts and laments. They crept to the hut unseen. First, Ganga put the child in bed and rocked her to sleep silently. She got up and groped for the loom, but she knew without seeing that it had been broken into many pieces and that she would never hear its music again. She was certain that her tapestries were missing. Burned, torn, or stolen, she did not know, but she knew that they were gone. She cried until her bandages were soaked and heavy and loose. Her eyes burned.

She peeled off her bandages carefully. She felt the swollen sockets with her fingers, making sure that nothing had been damaged. Then she opened her eyes very slowly. The bright light stabbed her eyeballs. She gasped at the pain and the brightness, and closed them again. The sun had stung her like lye.

When she opened them again after a while, she saw that the world was out of focus and that rainbows streamed from all the objects that came into her line of vision. Her eyes brimmed with tears. She walked out of the hut, clutching at the walls as she felt her way to the acacia tree. From under its spiky shade, she peered into the place where the youth had dug the trench for the foundation of the palace. She thought she saw a rat scurry near something pink that stared up glassily at her from under the mud, but she could not be sure. She wiped her eyes.

She gazed at the world around her, whose details now seemed to be sharper and crueller in the pitiless sunlight than she could ever recall. Then, shading her eyes with her hand, she walked to the others who were moving unsurely in their darkness like wind-up toys. One by one, they told her that they had all lost their sight, but could see clearly how they had lost something that was even more valuable. She turned in the direction of the sound of that mocking music, which was fading in the distance, and imagined that she saw the blur of a figure with a bulging sack, pedalling away. She knew that, although she could see, she was truly blind now.

From every hut came the sound of crying.

HAPPINESS AND **O**THER DISORDERS

I've just changed from my walking shorts into a suit, and we're on our way in a taxi to the banquet hall, watching schoolchildren with bags drinking that root beer that tastes of Dettol, eating ice cream, with cellphones and earphones, they'll run out of ears there, and she says what about it, did we bring any, and I ask, what janno, presents, she says, the stuff Hina sent, and I go, no, that's back there, but I have the money, that would be enough for now, after all he's a student, he'll take a cheque, he can put it to use, setting up house, presents can wait, fine, she says with a sniff, if that's how you feel, money, it's your nephew's engagement, for god's sake, there is such a thing as an occasion, I wonder aloud what she's like, he hasn't said much about her, this Milada, probably some pasty Czech from Brno fed on potatoes, without the benefit of sun, when suddenly there's Tariq with a newly minted moustache, all ninety pounds of him, in a bush shirt and a tuxedo, peering in at the taxi window, I exclaim and bound out to hug him, while she's paying off the cab, he says mamoojan, although it should be khaloojan, how nice, this is Milada, let me introduce you, my favourite uncle, doesn't say his only uncle, bless him, next to him, his fiancée, but boy, was I wrong, she doesn't fit into my field of vision no matter how I try, and, before I know it, I am gripped, breathless, by two white arms large as windmill blades, cutting off my sight and squeezing the life out of me, ah how nice, Milada, I manage to squeak, goodness, I've gained a niece-in-law, what a one, I try hugging back and puckering up for some suavum, when she falls over, or rather I tilt back, knees all buckled with the sheer joy of it, and she falls on top of me, my breath knocked out of me with a whoosh like a bellows, luckily the ground was soft, but I swear I was out for a few minutes, Houston, that was some crash landing, when I woke up to my wife's screams, Sami, are you all right, Sami, don't die on me, Sami, not in this country, and then it's much dusting and brushing of grass and leaves and some tittering but I am stunned and still prone, but my wife is all collected now and hissing, okay, now, Sami, get up for god's sake, you're making a scene, trust you, and I say I can't, my back's gone, but look, if you want to give it to Tariq and that huge wife of his, the money's in my back pocket, here, put your hand in, but now she is boiling, whistling, spitting like a kettle, you know they're not married, and I won't, Sami, you do this every time, and I say never, when was the last time I fell over after being suffocated by a human airbag, but she goes on, people can hear you, but that's good, I think, see, so maybe now someone can help me up, which you're not likely to do, and they come and they do, hoist me by my legs and shoulders, some dinner jackets, frilly tuxedos, aftershaves, and even an achkan, lay me out on the drinks table, between the merlots and chardonnays, it's agony, while Milada looms over me with concern, and my insides go liquid, never felt so helpless, and do all I can not to go goo goo at those grey eyes in that vast red face, asking me if I'm okay, I nod feebly, she is chewing something, swilling a quart of wine, this good ship Milada Hidayatullah, god, what a name-to-be, too much for him, at last she spreads her sails and drifts crosswind, ah, Tariq is imbibing too, but my wife is pretending not to notice, hsst, I call her, listen, janno, something, my ribs are probably cracked, it felt like an elephant squatted on me, how much do you think she weighs, and she goes, why, do you have problems breathing, and then, oh, shut up, Sami, of course, that's not funny, obesity is a disease in America, could be glandular, and I say, right, of course it is, feel I've just been bagged by an entire epidemic in one swoop, I feel squashed, she must come from a good family, I reckon drinks are out, so pass me some canapés, you know, he'll have to get on top if he's to get anywhere, and she is laughing and fuming at the same time, it was a sight though, really, Sami, why can't you behave, she really is very sweet and was so upset by the whole thing, try to get up, this really is the last straw, well, yes, of course it is, and consider this camel's back well and truly broken, oh fine, feel sorry for yourself, you rude, churlish *uncle*, she spat that out like an insult, oh, look, here's Raheela, my, is that Mona, god, how pretty and grown up and so serious, and then they all come in turns to inquire and, when that formula's done, nonchalantly pour out a drink behind my back, when I strain to rotate my eyes to the back, I can see my hair, all shiny, and hear the polite mutterings of concern, I feel a bit like a corpse at an Irish wake if one felt at all, then it's the gurgling and chinking and glugging, what are they having, ginger ale with scotch on the rocks, and wine and rum, god knows, and I am feeling giddy, with all that eye-swivelling and hand-shaking, that vision reappears, but I can't see her, I swear, she's like Chesterton's man Sunday whom the eye can't gird and mine are tired with all that moving about, saying something like *mummyjan*, but this time she's got a long cognac chub of goose liver, which she intends I bet to slather on that brick of Ryvita that she holds in her right, and I feel very faint at the enormity of this insight, when Tariq asks, shall I take you to the hospital, mamoojan, let me see if I can get a doctor first and, what do you know, there is one in the crowd, a jolly fat man, another diseased American, I suppose, ah, Mr. Sam (*Sam?*), we've had an accident I hear, have we, how sad, I ask, have you had one too, ah, you will jest, that's the spirit, let me see, and suddenly his fingers are digging pincer-sharp into my sides and spine, gah, felt that, good, no nerve damage then but we can't ever be too sure, can we, let me know if you have problems micturating, some bruising all over, I expect, does it hurt here and here and here, yes, of course, it bloody well hurts, leave my limbs alone, have that sack of bramborový potatoes fall on you like the grace of god and then ask that bloody damn-fool question, but I don't say that because you know what doctor's fingers are like, with too knowing of anatomy, it can be painful, we must eliminate all the possibilities and leave the probable, he says, however improbable that may be, yes, as the only possibility, Occam's razor, don't you know, not even a close shave, sounds like stinking, mangled Holmes to me but I am getting good at holding my peace, an X-ray and an MRI of the sacral and lumbar areas, good, good, I concur, probably just a severe mechanical strain on the spine, and I nod agreeably, I'll see if I can slip you a muscle relaxant or some codeine, and I say, doctor, can't you just inject some cognac intravenously without my wife knowing it, and he barks with delight, his red polka-dotted bow-tie bobbing in laughter along with the rest of him, very good, very good, here take this with some water, can you sit up, and when I try my back feels as if lacerated with red-hot tridents held no doubt in those voluminous arms, and I faint by and by before the music began and the in-laws came, so that was how it all started, mind you, I couldn't blame it all on Milada, I did go and see them three months later when they had settled into this apartment and I could walk up those flights of stairs on a day with the temperature in the high thirties, and I said I thought all the buildings in the USA had lifts and air-conditioning, and the good woman says I wish, and climbs and climbs, remembering all her mothers and grandmothers on the stairs, then we are up there, and knocking away, and she opens the door, which has a corn thing on it, our Milada, her face redder than I recalled, ah come in, Tareeeq will be back, just went out for some cigarettes, don't worry I won't hug you, and I joke, saying I'm better padded now, but my wife gave me one in the ribs which hurt, padding and all, and there aren't any windows, and the blasts hit me, first the Inagaddadavida and the smell of baking, so strong and so hot and airless, that I faint again and hit my head on the floor, but this time, I wake up with the smell of iodine on my cheek and Tariq fanning me with a newspaper with some headline about Reagan, and says in a clipped tone, I see that the heat from Milada's breakfast of brownies had taken its toll, well, I guess so it had, but, of course, my wife wouldn't see it that way, it's your flair for the theatrical, she said later, you should have been born a debutante in Victorian times, all done up tightly in a whalebone corset and you could have swooned away to glory, and I said, oh, that's good, read that somewhere, did you, and she says, look, I don't want to argue with you, and I say, who's arguing, I was just asking a question, a fair do for a bookish person to inquire into sources, and she says, a fair do, who speaks like that, what will they think, fainting like that and all, it's an act or an insult, I'm not sure which, look, I'm sorry, truly sorry but I couldn't help it, okay fine, I say exasperatedly, tell Hina that I had a fit of the vapours like Widow Twankey and Tariq revived me with some smelling salts, just like Aladdin, but her eyes began to glisten, look, let's invite them over, I say hastily, we have an exhaust, AC, windows, lifts, the lot, and I'll make my chicken biryani, janno, and you can do the rest, okay, she relents, let's do it next week, and they come, or she does, for I have eyes for no one else, billowing into the room, with all the force of creation, blocking out the fireplace and everything else, including Tariq who is folded into some corner, but I try not to look while Tariq is talking about stocks and about his research over the eggs benedict arnold, her dish that turns on you, and Milada about her work in the hospital where she had met him when he was suffering from anaemia, when my wife brings out the chumchums and rasgollas and I go weak, not for me, janno, since my back, I haven't been able to cut down on those twenty-six pounds, you know what the doctor says about Mr. Sam, and my *ur*-niece says, *mummyjan*, I can resist everything except temptation, wish I had your willpower, and I watch fascinated like whatever animal it is that watches a stoat, taken with this life force not a bit sickened, unlike the time on the New York subway where this woman held a big pizza and wheeled it as she nibbled the sides right to the core, which she gulped down like a dog without chewing, all without taking a breath, an efficient eating machine, or, as we would say, mashallah, but that had put me off food for days, the gluey masticated paste slithering down the old peristaltic tube, coating it with spittle, breaking it down into a bolus for bacteria to eat some of it, the saliva mashing the chyle and chyme, it was sheer gluttony, but this is elemental and cosmomorphic, there's grace, beauty too, it enthralls me until I feel another sharp elbow in my sides, god, I have been bruised all over on this trip, and Milada is now talking about how she misses the ovocné knedlíky, fruit dumplings, that they used to make, aswim in cottage cheese and butter, at the Hotel Pegas, and then tells us this dream she just had where she is out in the meadow or a glade, she isn't sure of the word, picking daisies, hears the drone overhead, watches the plane drop something, and puts out her hand and catches the bomb, except that it's a boiled egg, anyway, that's how it all began, all these aches and pains, boy, was I ever glad to get back to India, of course, the back has persisted, and my janno's father sent me his old masseur's son, who came on his Vespa wearing an army cap and fatigues, and smelling of rose attar, and I asked him, look, I had this problem in the States and the doctors there tell me that it's deep-tissue trauma, are you familiar with Swedish or deep-tissue massage, yes, sir, yes, sir, of course, of course, he says, grooming his moustache with a tiny comb, Swedish, Russian, and English massage, any type, even Hungarian and Bulgarian and Serbo-Croatian, so why don't we go into your bedroom, *hello, what's this, my bedroom*, and when I am there, locks it and says, please lie...face down, oh, this all right, I ask, yes, good, says the Swedorussoanglomagyar masseur, please take off your top, good, my father was Hidayatsahib's barber and masseur, he used to massage all his brothers too after their cricket matches, very famous sportsmen, all five dead now, just in their thirties, sad, I go every week now, his father was like my father, and when he used to scold me, I used to really like it, and please now untie your pajamas and roll them down, down, down, *eh*, say I, *what are you doing?* sir, everything is connected, if I touch something down there, then, sir, it helps something else up here, in that case, I say, please try to grab the connection from the top not from the bottom, er, I mean, not from down there, let me hitch them up, OK, sir, I liked chemistry best in school, sir, carbon-carbon double-bond, how do you like my oil, I make it myself, very good, I say, very excellent indeed, although to me it looked and smelled just like Vicks, it's my own secret formula, says this man, but I make just 15,000 rupees a day between my three clinics, I know you've been to America where they make much more, I ask him, were you in the army and when he says no, I say but the cap is very nice, oh, fashion, sir, from film with Shahrukh Khan, he says, Fendi, how much for it in the U of SA, I'll be damned if I know but I cite an astronomical sum and he looks pleased, look, I have a bad injury, you have to get through several layers of muscle, and he asks, sir, do you exercise and I tell him I try to, and he goes, sir, sir, you are doing it all wrong, all, all wrong, the muscles are all wrong, okay, fine, I got that, well, do what you can, I have several knots which you need to press down on until they give up, but he says no, sir, I don't think I should press down, nerve damage, I don't do that, never, never, never, so I ask him what he intends doing for the next forty-five minutes, and he says give me three weeks and you'll be fighting fit, but I am losing my temper, look, the problem is deeper, I need some relief right now, and tickling me won't help, and he is off again, it must be a good life in America, and I say, no, they don't have any windows or air-conditioning in America, and he says hard to believe but maybe because of the snow in the U of SA and maybe all movie sets only, I say, yes, and the women are enormous and go to gas bars where they blow them up and can he please do the knots like I said, but he insists on me trying his method which is when I ask him caustically, *what, patty-cake caresses, eh,* sir, sir, please, he entreats, sir, don't exercise in that way, I'll come tomorrow, sir, so I give him the money, cursing, as I head off to the bath, and he asks me how much a masseur earns in America, and I tell him that with his amazing techniques, particularly the Hungarian manoeuvres, he can make this outlandish wage, and he goes away preening his moosh, dreaming of gas bars and vast bodies oiled with VapoRub, while I ask my wife to make sure that when he comes again, to tell him that I have gone out for a walk or am asleep, and I spend most mornings hiding from him which of course delights my janno who imitates the *brum-brum* of a scooter whenever she's making the omelette for breakfast, har de bloody har, but I don't say anything because my little Mount Etna says when you're in that mood, Sami, you're not at all phonogenic, not in the least, always with the last word